Deliver Us From Evil

Demons Beware Book II

By Mike Evans

Please don't forget to leave a **<u>REVIEW</u>**! Authors rely on <u>you</u>, the reader, to help widen their audience through word of mouth and feedback. Getting stars and good reviews helps us on our way. Thank you for reading!

Thanks to my beta readers Karen, Leslie, Jon, Denise, Ricky, Matthew, & Rosa. You guys are wonderful!

Please look for me on Facebook

Mike's Newsletter sign up
http://tinyurl.com/evansnewsletter

Mike Evans Fan Club Page Facebook
https://www.facebook.com/groups/1523345561293296/

M. Evans' Author Page on Facebook
https://www.facebook.com/pages/M-Evans-Author/1438259789750360

Mike Evans Author Website
http://mevansm01.wix.com/mikeevansauthor

Contact Email
m.evansauthor@gmail.com

Mike Evans on Amazon
http://www.amazon.com/Mike-Evans/e/B00IQ9Z75A

Books by Mike Evans

<u>The Orphans Series</u>
The Orphans: Origins Vol I
Surviving the Turned Vol II (The Orphans Series)
Strangers Vol III (The Orphans Series)
White Lie Vol IV (The Orphans Series)
<u>Civil War Vol V (The Orphans Series)</u>
<u>Divided Vol VI (The Orphans Series)</u>

<u>Gabriel Series</u>
Gabriel: Only one gets out alive
Pitch Black (Gabriel Book 2)
Body Count (Gabriel Book 3)

<u>The Uninvited Series</u>
The Uninvited Book 1
The Stranger Book II of The Uninvited series
The Unwelcomed Book III of The Uninvited Series

Buried: Broken oaths

Voices in My Head

<u>Demons Beware</u>
Demons Beware Book 1
Deliver Us From Evil Book II of Demons Beware

Deal With the Devil

Zombies and Chainsaws

Dark Roads Book II of Zombies and Chainsaws

This book is dedicated to Christy Thornbrugh. One of the most special and difficult things as an author is growing close to your readers. Unfortunately, life can be too short and often people don't get the chance to do everything that they aspire to. She was a wonderful human being that I will miss dearly and if I have learned one thing from her passing it is to live life to the fullest each day.

The Devil never sleeps, he does not stop planning, nor does he quit. He plans and he waits. Time is unimportant to beings that do not expire. They simply pick and choose when to execute their plans, with the hope that one day they will slip past those who are destined to protect the living. This is a demonic story and the Devil has come for blood.

Chapter 1

Hoyt Hotel Presidential Suite – Las Vegas, NV 1988

CEO Williams Room.

Jack Brown sat in the dark closet checking his watch and shaking his head, disgusted at how long he had been in there. A laughing came from down the hallway from someone who was either beating the house or who had been drinking all night in one. The keys to the room jingled until a curse word finally came and he slid in the key, twisting the lock open. The man flicked on the light to the bedroom suite walking around. Jack knew the sound of chips hitting the counter and this man had just unloaded a bundle of them.

Jack watched through the crack in the door of the closet as the man shimmied out of a high-end suit coat that any cowboy would be proud to wear. He tossed his black Stetson cowboy hat on the bed and fell on it trying to get his leg up high enough to get his cowboy boots off, but his substantial gut was causing an issue and keeping it from happening. In an accent that left little question of if he was from Texas or not he yelled, "Oh for hell's sake would you get off my foot you stupid damn boot!"

The man's face had turned almost purple from the work put into the task and he looked like it was going to burst from the strain. A button shot off his shirt and across the room. "Christ, Helen is going to notice that one, maybe one of them girls down in the tailor's office can fix this."

He lifted both legs as high as he could and brought them both down quickly trying to use the momentum to get to his feet. The unmistakable sound of a tear echoed through the large room. He patted at his ass, feeling nothing but boxers at the bottom of his crotch. He undid the giant belt buckle rolling to his side thinking of many documentaries he'd seen over his lifetime and beached whales came to mind.

The man finally made it to his feet only to fall over onto his face on the floor with a large thud. Jack couldn't stand the carnival show anymore, he opened the closet door slowly stepping out. Other than a pair of pants and a stained wife-beater muscle shirt there was nowhere that a weapon could be placed. Jack walked up slowly, pistol in one hand and a heavy gauge guitar string that he'd attached to two small pieces of wood, one that had a hook so he could tighten the noose with the other. The man tried to sit up, but had the same results as before.

"Would you please stop. I'm almost beginning to feel bad for you. You have issues you know that?"

The man tried to rush away but Jack kicked his feet out from under him sending him back into a pushup position. Williams yelled, "Who in the hell are you? What are you doing in my hotel room?"

"It seems your wife doesn't like you very much, Mr. Williams. I won't lie, I'm a little surprised that you have got a wife in the first place. Were you rich when you met her?"

"What does that mean?"

"Sir, I've had bowel movements that are more graceful and better looking than you. What I mean is, I don't think you would have a chance in hell of getting a wife if it wasn't motivated financially, unless you are hung like a horse, which...I honestly don't see it. I really don't," Jack said shrugging his shoulders.

"Helen wouldn't kill me, she loves me, she's waiting for me to come home tonight, she'll be worried sick if I don't make it home. I swear to God."

"Uh huh, well I'm not a big believer in the man upstairs and you live in Dallas, Texas. If you had any plans about being home tonight, then you would have left six hours ago. Do you have any idea how long I've been waiting for you to come back? You should have been back hours ago."

Williams in his drunken stupor finally realized what the man was holding. He tried to get back, but was too drunk and too fat to get up from where he was lying. "What are you going to do with that?"

Jack held up the pistol. "This is if you scream, I'll just shoot you in the head and make it quick. This is to make you suffocate, make your neck bleed, make your eyes pop out of your head and probably make you shit yourself."

"Why would you use that?"

"Helen really doesn't like you! I'm not talking about a little bit; we are talking a lot. I asked her how she would like me to take care of you; she just said to make sure it hurts. Now I'm usually a nice guy, people tend to like me...not those that I am killing, but waitresses, bartenders, those types of people, I'm a great tipper, a really nice guy."

"I can pay you, I can-"

"She said that you'd tell me that, that you would lie too, that you'd flee town, and that you don't have access to the money just the horrible decisions that you make for your company. She wanted me to tell you, you deserve this."

Jack took the man by the hair tightly holding him, letting it slide to the back of his neck so he could place the loop to the string around it. Williams started clawing at Jack's wrists. As Jack looked down he could see Williams was trying to get free. He knelt next to the man and Williams was still trying to grab his wrists as he was attempting to tighten the string around the man's neck. "You shouldn't do that, it's rude."

Williams was trying to put up a fight, even as pathetic as it was. Jack looked down smiling. The man made a horrible mistake and punched Jack in the mouth. Blood ran down his chin, the man smiled and Jack did too licking the blood off his hand.

When he tried swinging again, Jack took his wrist, more than ready. He wrapped his hand around it bringing it down with such force that he snapped it in two, the bone came out and the pain was so great that Williams choked only a peep aloud.

Tears filled Williams' eyes as Jack took the man's other hand and patted it softly, looking at it before repeating and getting the same result. His blood began to pool on the floor on either side of him. Jack whispered in his ear as the man tried to scream, the pain was so bad that he was unable to utter a sound. "You aren't going to try touching me again, are you?"

The man shook his head no, as his lips quivered. He took a good hold of the wood end of the choker. "It's only going to hurt...until you die."

Jack sat behind him putting his heels on the man's shoulders, holding the wood tight and pulled back until a thin line began to grow from the fat rolls on his sweat-drenched neck. Jack pulled until white foam appeared in the man's mouth as he began to convulse and his legs kicked wildly. Jack undid the noose around his neck the crimson colored blood dripped down. He used the man's shirt to wipe it off checking his pulse and making sure there would be no worry about him coming back. He took a handful of chips as he left thinking this would be his lucky night.

Chapter 2

Las Vegas two hours later - 1988

Jack sat outside of his apartment building smoking a cigarette tapping the ash on the wet road beneath. He rubbed his free hand through his black cropped hair before deciding he'd waited long enough. Jack had been sitting there for an hour watching his window from the street. Jack had been in the business of killing people for over a decade. He knew that with every kill, there could always be repercussions, but he always did his best to be careful, smart and made sure he was always paid. It wasn't the targets that scared him, it was people who'd paid him to do it and to hitters that wanted to be number one.

He took the last few hits on his smoke, deciding that, yes, it was safe to enter. He rolled up his window and looked around. It had been raining recently and that wasn't something normal for a city that barely ever saw precipitation. The only thing it was abundant with was sin and sinners and that was the way he liked it. The calls from home to work out of New York had come regularly, but he'd denied all of them knowing that Vegas was now his home.

Jack took the steps slowly. He'd waited in his last job's home for forty-eight hours, waiting for him to come home. The window that he'd been given was loose and by the time the man had come home, he was half tempted to go after the contract instigator. He could feel his pistol bouncing against his ribs as he walked up the steps. Most people would find it annoying, but he loved the security of knowing it was there when and if he needed it.

Jack didn't see anyone in the stairways, it was only midnight and most of the residents worked on the strip and wouldn't be home until after the bars had shut down or in some cases until the sun had begun to come up. He slid in the key turning it slowly, being in a hurry was what kept people from having any longevity in the business and he damn well knew that. Jack opened it only an inch and ran a knife, blunt side, down the door crack. It stopped on the fishing string he'd strung across the door. Each time his knife hit that it was as soothing as anything he'd ever felt. He was never off guard, but he also never took for granted a good night's sleep.

Jack stepped in pulling off his suit coat and took a hangar off the wall doing it all in the dark. He didn't need light to know where things were in his apartment. Jack kept everything where it needed to be for that simple purpose. He walked over to the kitchen finally turning on the light above the stove. He pulled out an inch-thick manila envelope filled with hundred-dollar bills. He thought once he hit two million dollars that he would only pull triggers if it meant his own protection and this would add another ten grand to it.

He undid the holster that strapped across his chest and slid off his rig setting the heavy forty-five-caliber and the twenty-two caliber pistols on the kitchen table and rolled his shoulders enjoying the weight being gone and pulling at the dress shirt where the sweat had soaked through. Jack brought out a tumbler, skipping the ice and pouring two fingers of Jack Daniels. He smelled it licking his lips as his mouth began to salivate wanting very badly for its treat to be consumed.

A voice cleared its throat from behind him. Jack took the silenced twenty-two caliber pistol in his right hand spinning around not bothering to remove the holster; they unlike him could be replaced. He fired off four shots, the silencer, illegal of course kept the noise from echoing through the building, not that he was worried about narcs in the apartment.

The men he worked for had most of the police covered, especially those working the shit neighborhoods that he lived in on purpose. Jack saw a shadow in the dark jolt four times, one for each shot. He held the pistol never letting it fall, he hit the light just in time to see a man standing in his living room, he blinked, trying to make sense of it because his brain and eyes were on opposite ends of what he was looking at. Jack whispered, "What in God's name?"

The intruder had not fallen, nor had he looked like he was going to. Jack flipped on another light as he walked over cautiously. He half expected him to be stuck on something and only a hook was keeping the man on his feet.

The voice came back sounding foreign but Jack was clueless as to where it originated from. "Good Evening, Mr. Brown."

Jack aimed point-blank for the man's chest. He'd been killing long enough, he knew that headshots were too easy to miss, but at the same time was wondering if there might be a bulletproof vest that he was wearing. "How do you know my name?"

"Well, Jack, I could call you Scott Canners if you want me to be accurate. But we both know that you don't go by that name anymore."

Jack smiled squeezing the trigger one more time. The gun jumped and he had to blink to take in what he was truly seeing. The last of the bullets from his pistol were stuck three inches in front of his pistol spinning in the air as if it was still rotating coming out of the barrel. Jack let his arm and the pistol drop to his side, "What are you, some kind of magician? Do you know what I can do to people; I got a reputation in this town?"

The man walked up closer out of the shadows. Jack took a step back as the thin-lipped smiling man walked toward him. Jack could see his shots had very much found a home and they'd gone all the way through. If the man owned a bulletproof vest, he was most definitely not wearing it this evening. Four tightly grouped holes were in his chest. A slow flow of blood trickled from the bullet holes. The man reached forward with his index finger and thumb taking the bullet from midair.

"No, I am no magician, however, they do fascinate me. I would say they made a deal with the devil to be able to do what it is they can pull off but I know that isn't true."

Jack was swimming through a million thoughts. Absolutely nothing made sense about what he was thinking and what was going on tonight. "Then how are you doing that?"

The man ran his hands up and down in this old thing kind of a fashion. He stuck his fingers in the holes, pulling them out covered in blood. Jack raised the pistol one more time not hesitating to aim point-blank at the man's skull and pulled the trigger. His head snapped back, brains and blood covered the back of the wall. The man did not fall, though, Jack stepped forward, "What in God's name?"

The man brought his head back down, a single drop of blood ran down his nose and a small hole that expanded to the size of a golf ball in the rear of his head was now present.

"I think you might have the wrong ruler in mind, Jack, my boy."

Jack spun on his heel pushing off to run. His feet went out from under him and he looked down to see that he was no longer on the hardwood floors of his apartment. The stranger lifted his finger, bringing him closer with one motion of his finger. Jack started screaming but the man closed his index and thumb together and with that his mouth shut as well. The man walked up slowly doing a little dance that reminded him of every tap dance act he'd ever seen Sinatra do on the strip. He tried to move but was paralyzed from the neck down.

The intruder got within whispering distance to him. "Do I have your attention? Are you scared yet? I am not known for my patience. Are you getting an idea of who you are dealing with yet, Jack?"

Jack tried to nod but couldn't. The man lowered his hand dropping him on the ground where he landed on his back hard, grunting through his clenched lips. He opened his fingers, letting him breathe and speak again. "What do you want? Are you a demon?"

"No, I am not a demon, I tried that once and it didn't work out so well," the man pointed up to the roof. "You know who had to interfere and ruin all of my fun. I was so close but he just doesn't see eye to eye with me. We were friends once, before he sent me to rule hell. Now I have a new plan and you are going to help me."

"I am not doing anything for you. You're crazy!"

"How much proof do you need, Jack, to prove to you that I am who I say I am? What if I cut my head off and then spoke, or maybe you'd like me to take you to hell with me, show you around? There are some real interesting people I could introduce you to. You know it doesn't have to be all that bad. It is better to come with an invitation, than to be sent there because of the sins you have collected throughout your life. I assure you that you have got all of the sins one needs for a red-carpet invitation to hell."

"You can't afford me."

"You still think money is important? I thought that you were much brighter than this. I could possess you, I could take you over, but then that'd just ruin everything. I need a pure human, well as pure as you could be expected to be since you are a killer."

"I don't want to go to hell, I -"

"You will do as I say, or I will rip you apart and eat your soul. If you are worried about payment you may live like a king until you join me in your forever home, then you are a fool, but once you complete your task you'll live like a king for as long as money has meaning."

The man held out his hand, letting gold rain on the floor. Jack had never seen so much in his entire life. He watched in awe until his living floor was covered ankle deep in it. "What...what is it that you want me to do?"

"That's the spirit Jacky," and Satan went to pull a list from his pocket, realizing his fingers were still covered in blood. "You won't be able to read anything if I don't wipe this heart and blood off my fingers, now will you? I want to start stateside; the other countries are much more religious and faithful. I just love all of you sinners in the states. Do you know what an exorcism is?"

"Yeah, it's where priests send the damned back to hell where-"

"Careful, Jack, you wouldn't want to offend me, would you?"

"No, of course not."

"There are a handful here in the USA, a few close, a few far away, I need you to help me with them."

"You need me to kill them? So, you can come up here, with whatever it is that you have down there, is that it?"

"Yes, Jack, try not to sound so high and mighty, it is better to have me as a friend."

Jack looked at the window thinking of the four stories to the pavement below. He thought that maybe God would show him mercy if he lied and leapt to his death. Satan was in his head lifting him back off the ground. "You might like to know that there were ten before you. I am sure that you have not had a lot of competition from those that you consider either better or in the same class as yourself. Is that the truth?"

"It's been quiet from others lately. Do I have you to thank for that?"

"They are dead because they took the moral high road, don't worry, they are still in hell, he was above mercy and they ended up exactly where they belonged. I assure you an invitation to hell is much better than a punishment. You kill these priests and when my reign on Earth begins you will never want for another thing again. But you must make it look like an accident."

"Because you fear that he will step in and send you back to hell, is that it?"

"See, you aren't as stupid as you look. Yes, I'd like to try and not deal with him, he always ruins everything good. Now do we have a deal, or would you like me to do to you what I did to the others who have turned me down?"

Jack looked at the window again and Satan finally lost what little patience he had. He stuck one finger to Jack's skull, sending each of the ten assassins into his mind at one time. He saw one being burned alive, the skin being peeled off a man he knew and had worked with named Jesus, another being boiled to death in water and those were the tame ones. When he lifted his finger, Jack knew that he had no choice. Satan leaned in so close that his lips were brushing his ear. "Remember, you cannot get away, you cannot run, you cannot hide, and if you kill yourself I will be seeing you even sooner than you want."

"But how do I get hold of you if I need your help?"

"You just think of me Jack, and I will be here as quickly as I can."

"Really?"

"No, Jack, kill them, if you don't I'm going to kill you and make what I did to the others look like a sweet dream. Do you understand me? Any questions you have, Jack?"

"Kill priests, go to hell either way, but live like a king and have an invitation, is that about the gist of things?"

"You got it, Jack."

Jack gazed at the gold and Satan disappeared. Leaving only the corpse, it fell to the gold dirtying it with its blood. Jack pushed up from the ground, rubbing at his hair that was soaking wet and his heart was racing like he had never before experienced. He crawled over to the man shaking him, but it was lifeless. He rested against the couch holding up his hand in front of him only to see them shake. He took long, deep breaths until he could keep them still. It was far from his first body that he'd ever seen but had never put a bullet through one and had it come back before. He crawled over to the phone, picking it up, dialing the number and waiting for it to answer. "I've got a broken water heater I'd like to be fixed."

"Is the unit disabled?"

"Understatement."

"Will this be cash or charge, sir?"

Jack held up a handful of the gold smiling lightly, he realized there were thousands of the coins. "Gold and I need it now, double your usual service charge if you can get here in the next twenty minutes. Is that going to be an issue?"

"We wouldn't want to keep you waiting, Mr.?"

"Just get here, top floor and now."

Jack pushed up to his feet going straight to the bathroom. He ripped the shower curtain off its hooks and packaged his delivery. He did his best getting the coins where no one would see them and pushed the corpse out into the kitchen, leaving a stack of five coins on his chest. Jack got up walking for his gear and looking at where the address he needed to go to was located. "California, here I come."

Chapter 3

Parker House

Tony slapped the alarm clock when it started beeping. He didn't want to wake up his mother before she had to be ready for work. He sat up in bed scratching his back and running his hands through his hair. He rolled out of bed, getting the motivation to go to the shop and have yet another day full of turning wrenches and working on people's cars who could barely afford to fix them. He was thankful for the work, it was hard, but it was honest and steady and that wasn't something that most in the neighborhood could attest to having the opportunity to say they had.

He cracked the window and lit up a smoke. He thought about showering, but knew he was just going to get dirty again at work. He could shower at his girlfriend's, Alecia, if he got off before she had to be at the diner. He watched the street, it looked abandoned at this time of the day or more like a war zone. Broken liquor bottles in the street, cars that people couldn't afford to fix on the curb and with the exception of a few lights coming on from other homes in the neighborhood it was still dark as night. He turned on his lamp and it flickered giving him the creeps.

A voice whispered, but he couldn't hear it well enough, he thought with as thin as the walls were that maybe it was the neighbors fighting, which didn't make a lick of sense to him at five in the morning. He looked down at his smoke, watching it being sucked into his closet. He took a hold of his work shirt slamming the door loudly and sticking a chair underneath it.

He had hated this room ever since he was four years old for given reasons. His mother had wanted to move them out, but with the loss of his father or lack thereof as no one actually knew what became of him she could just barely afford to keep a roof over their heads. He cringed at the noise, knowing if his mom wasn't already up that she surely was now. He slid on a pair of jeans and slung the shirt over his shoulder walking down the steps. His mother's room was still dark and he thanked the lord he hadn't awoken her.

He slipped down the steps seeing the light was already on. Joan, his mother, was turning on the gas stove and Tony could already smell the coffee starting to brew. "Sorry I woke you ma, I was trying to be quiet."

"What was that loud noise upstairs? I thought maybe you'd fallen."

"I…I heard a voice in my room, it freaked me out. It was probably just my head playing tricks on me, I don't want you worrying about me."

"It's a mother's job to worry, Anthony Parker."

"You didn't have to make me breakfast, I could have gotten something on my way to the shop this morning."

"Please, there's nothing open at this ungodly hour. The last thing you need to do is go to work without anything on your stomach. It's a shock to me at all that the wind doesn't blow you over as thin as you are."

He smiled, kissing her on the back of the head. "That's why I have the motorcycle Ma, it keeps me weighed down."

"It's a death trap and I wish you'd get rid of that thing. I think the only reason young boys buy those is to give their mothers heart attacks. I don't know why you can't just buy a normal car, or take the bus."

"The bus doesn't run this time of morning and the last thing I can afford is a car, even though I could at least fix it now if I ever came across one in halfway decent condition."

Tony took a seat looking at the pile of mail on the table neatly organized into his and her piles. He looked through some junk mail, a few motorcycle magazines, until he came to a golden envelope with the name of his church and a cross in the return corner. "That came for you yesterday, Tony. If you kept decent hours, maybe a mother would see you a little more often than she does."

"It isn't my fault, I got too much on my plate right now."

"You have too much on your plate. Just because we live down in the slums does not mean we need to talk like one. Now eat your eggs before they get cold, that mail can wait."

"It's from the church, the letter I sent in to inquire about being a priest."

Joan stopped plating the eggs and set them down on a hot pad on the table. "Well, why are you sitting there, why don't you open it?"

He wanted to say something smart, but nothing he could think of to say would leave him with anything but a slap upside the back of the head. "What was I thinking?"

Tony ripped the envelope open trying not to look too eager. He was confident that he was doing a horrible job. He pulled it out and saw catalogs for the diocese in Chicago. He looked up to his mom and his and her lips both quivered a little. He read the letter seeing that he had been accepted. Tears were hitting the paper as he read and his mother wasn't doing any better job controlling her emotions. He showed her the paper and the smile she had melted away instantly. "What, I thought, I thought you were happy, I thought you would be happy for me, mom?"

She set the letter down gently, smoothing it and remembering something very similar when Billy had applied to the church, which was more of a formality than anything given everything he'd done already. "I would be happy, Tony, I mean I am, it's just that I think there was a mistake, honey."

Tony ripped the paper off the table. "What do you mean there was a-"

Tony dropped the paper back down on the table. The name Howard Plum stared back at him in the recipient's name. His shoulders slouched and his hope started to dwindle. That feeling of getting out of the shop and being able to do something positive for the community and the world for that matter and people's beliefs very quickly melted away. "I thought...I thought that I got in, I thought that after this many times applying they would grant me a meeting."

"It was just a mistake, don't hold it against them for too long, okay, Tony, I know it hurts. I wish I had something good to say but this really is horrible. Is there anything I can do for you?"

"No, but I'm going to call Father Michaels at lunch, maybe he can see about getting me a meeting. I'd like to know if I am in or not. I can be doing someone else a good deed by letting them know they sent it to the wrong place. I only hope that he deserves to be a priest."

Joan got up, giving him a hug and holding him tight for a moment. "If you don't get in then it just means that God had greater things in mind for you. I know how bad you want this and I am sure that Father Michaels would be happy to help you in any way that he can."

Chapter 4

St Mary's Cathedral, Los Angeles

The phone rang on the head priest's desk. He looked at it for a moment wondering who was running a raffle this week that they needed help with. He picked it up and said, "Good afternoon, this is Father Edward, how may I help you?"

"Edward old friend, it is Father Michaels out of Chicago. How are you?"

"Oh no, what happened."

"Do I always call with bad news, Edward?"

Edward ran through the last few years debating his answer. "Yes, yes, you always call with some sort of horrible news. Why is that, why can't you just call to say hi, old friend?"

"Well hello, Edward, how are you?"

"You're really just calling to say hi, Father Michaels, oh now I feel like a jackass, I'm sorry. I'm doing quite well, I've had a cold and these bunions will be the death of me but we are good. How are you?"

"Healthy as a horse, by chance are you alone?"

"No, I've got your two favorite young priests in the chapel saying prayers. Did you want to speak to Father Nathaniel or Carter?"

"I need to speak to both of them actually, I have a job for them."

Father Edward shook his head mumbling, "I thought you said, oh, never mind, you'll be the death of me, Father Michaels. Be patient, my old bones don't get out to the chapel as quickly as they once did. I could send a nun, but I fear they are in even worse shape than myself. I don't know when they will retire, but we could use someone younger."

"That's very nice Edward, could you please go get them now, this is quite important I assure you."

"It's always important, do you know what happens to me each time that I go out into the chapel to tell them they have work? Guilt, nothing but guilt. I don't know how to get around it."

"You need to have more faith, Father Edward. You think that you are punishing them in some way, but they are two of the few...two of the chosen, and they are doing more good than any of us could possibly imagine. Think what it means to take one of the demons and send them back to hell where they belong."

"Losing them would make me feel no better. I know that God would rest them in his hand and deliver them from evil, but it still makes me worry for them. You hold on, if you keep me talking, you'll never get a hold of them. They need cordless phones or more than one so we don't have to go running all around the church grounds trying to find someone to tell them there's a call."

"Cordless phones, yes, that is one invention I don't think we will see in our lifetime. Now, please I am truly in a hurry. I fear the devil is making a play, one that I think we should stop quite quickly."

Father Edward pushed up out of his plush seat. His knees and back both protested, but he forced himself upwards until he was standing tall. He patted his gut, one that was very healthy from a many number of church meals from his congregation. He always loved going to the homes where he could see how his flock behaved and lived outside of the house of God. The only thing that he feared going to the homes were the size of the meals. Not once could he remember, even when he was still a priest in training, that he received an invitation for anything less than that of what appeared to be a feast prepared for an army or Thanksgiving dinner.

Father Edward made his way down the hall. Putting an arm up against the wall every so often to steady himself and wishing that he still had the knees of a twenty-year-old man. By the time he got to the chapel his face was beet red. He opened the door, seeing the two priests on their knees, heads down, reciting prayers and speaking to the man upstairs.

Nathaniel looked up first seeing the head priest. He tapped Carter on the shoulder and held up a hand for Father Edward, he could see from where he was that he didn't need to go walking any further without worry of falling over.

Edward smiled resting against the doorframe. They made a sign of the cross as they exited, kneeling quickly as they left the pew. Father Carter put an arm under his elbow, helping him in and to a seat. "Father Edward, did you have something that bad that you needed to confess?" Carter joked.

Edward tried to smile and say something back, but waved it away, he didn't have the breath to joke around with. "Be quiet please and listen. Michaels...Father Michaels is on the phone; he has a job for the two of you."

Nathaniel and Carter sat him down in the pew patting him on the shoulder. "We'll go get the call. I think we need to get a second line or something, Father Edward."

"You are telling me that, hurry up, heaven knows how long that took me, he probably thinks I keeled over in the hallway. The two of you be careful, be smart, and take care of yourselves, and each other."

"We will and thank you for caring so much, Father Edward, we really appreciate you," Carter said.

They ran down the hall to the phone, Nathaniel rounded the corner first and sped into the office ahead of him. He took the phone first, plopping down into the office chair, leaving Carter standing in the doorway shaking his head. "You're getting old, Carter."

"I'm twenty-seven, Nathaniel, apparently you are getting senile in your old age because you're two years older than me."

"Yeah, but look at me, I come from good stock," Nathaniel replied.

"Nathaniel, would you please stop making Father Michaels wait. He doesn't call to chat."

Nathaniel cradled the phone and cleared his throat. "Hello, Father Michaels I-"

"I know for a fact that I've called you at least once to ask you about how things were going. I know for an absolute fact, because my memory is as good as they come. Do you think they'd have some half able minded priest running things for something this dangerous? No, no I don't suspect that they would."

"I'm sorry, I didn't mean whatever it is you heard. You were calling about a job that needed to be done, right?" Nathaniel questioned.

"Well of course I was, but it'd be nice if people didn't just assume that I am calling about something. Do you have a pen?"

Nathaniel took a piece of paper and pen from Edward's desk testing it and nodding. "Yes, sir, I do."

"I want you to go to 562 Elm Street in East Los Angeles. Mrs. Milton has been complaining that her son was starting to act a little funny to the bishop," Michaels ordered.

"Wow, she jumped right over the middleman, didn't she? Give us twenty minutes and we can head over there. Is she ready for us?"

"I can't say. I tried calling over there a few hours ago, multiple times and no one answered. You'll have to be the judge if she is there or not. Her teenage son is who they are having issues with," Father Michaels replied.

"Better than a kid, at least," Nathaniel replied.

"How is that?"

"At least a teen has lived a little, still a baby, but a four-year-old knows next to nothing."

"I guess, please report back to me and if you are lucky you'll be able to make noon mass," Michaels said with a tinge of fear in his voice, always worried about sending men to battle on behalf of others.

"Check, I'll call you this afternoon. I hope that it's a dumb demon, we could use one of those. They've been getting stronger and seeming like they have something going on, some reason why they have been wearing us down."

"Let's hope that isn't the case. They've made a play before for the world and it was less than desirable. The leftover demons took us months to eradicate but that is a story for a different day. Tell Mrs. Milton that we sent someone just as quickly as we could and apologize that we couldn't get someone sooner. I'm sure we'd like her to tell the bishop how well everything went, so let's try and make that a reality."

"Sooner I get off the phone sir, the quicker we will be on the way there," Nathaniel said carefully not wanting to offend his teacher and mentor.

"Right, go with God."

"As to you, sir, goodbye," Nathaniel replied replacing the phone back to its cradle.

Carter couldn't stand not being on the inside. "So, we do or we don't have a job?"

"We do have a job, Carter, and it isn't Father Michaels sending us to do it so much as he was directed by the bishop directly, they haven't been looked at and there's been no tests to see if it is psychological."

Carter whistled knowing that pulled some weight. He snatched the note looking where they were going and saw that there was some money where they were headed. "Looks like the demons take the possession without prejudice."

"How's that?" Nathaniel asked.

"They are in a rich neighborhood. They probably know the bishop very well or know someone who has a wing of a library named after them because of the donations they've given. I don't want to say that it is nice to know that the rich aren't any safer, I'm sure it would be looked at a bit sideways but it really is nice to know."

"Yeah, I can't say that I'm that keen on the idea personally," Nathaniel replied.

"I don't understand."

"Simple, rich people have money, money buys big houses."

"Right, Nathaniel and how does that matter?"

"It means that they probably have big houses, really big houses with really tall ceilings. The last thing I want to worry about is being taken up three or four stories and tossed out a window." Nathaniel said with hesitation in his voice.

Carter rubbed his back already thinking about the pain that would explode through it if such a thing happened. They went to their small dorm sized rooms gathering what they wanted to take with them on their persons and leaving the rest in their briefcases. When Nathaniel knocked on Carter's door, he was already waiting and held up a set of keys to a Buick. "We can take the church's car; I cleared it with Father Edwards already."

Chapter 5

Chicago 1988 – Hart Broadcasting Studios

Morty Spencer watched in the mirror of his dressing room as the young makeup artist got him prepped for air. "Mr. Spencer, I have been watching your show for years, I love it, I just absolutely adore it. You make me laugh so hard at some of the crazy people you have on."

"Did the producers talk to you today sweetheart about my guests we are having?"

"No, I'm sorry, should they have? It's my first day, I went nuts when they told me that I was going to get you ready today. Was there a special request you had, any suggestions?"

Morty smiled ear to ear tilting his head side to side looking at the bright lights on his face. He laughed his trademark laugh and his white veneers almost sparkled in the lights. "You see I was wondering if someone told you that maybe I was interviewing Gene Wilder today."

"Sir, I don't understand, I'm sorry."

"Well, I was just curious if you thought that making my face look like an Oompa Loompa might make good ol' Gene feel a little more at home here?"

"You think it's too orange?"

"No, I think it's great, do me a favor though, tell them to get your paycheck made up for you today on your way out."

She smiled awkwardly, "I swear I'll understand more on a normal basis."

Morty pulled the paper napkins from his shirt as he walked out to take the stage. "I'll let you know exactly what I mean. You are fired; you have a wonderful day, and maybe look for a new line of work."

Morty walked off to take his stage to interview the two priests that he had heard rumors over the last year that had been making their way around Chicago claiming to be taking those possessed by these so-called demons and sending them back to hell.

A knock came at the door to the dressing room provided to the show's guests. Father Michaels smiled poking his head in waving. "I had a call to make."

"Was it business, Father Michaels?" Billy Parker asked.
"It isn't always business when I call someone, you realize that, don't you? I don't think anyone realizes that. I talk; I do more than just work."

Father Michaels sat down on the visitor's couch, his frown turned into a smile as he watched the two boys as he tapped his ash in his hand. James watched, smiling, "You know, if you save that you could use it for lent, Father Michaels."

Billy was pacing back and forth. "You do realize that you've stuck us in a pool with a piranha, right? Spencer is going to put us through the ringer, Father Michaels" Billy said throwing his hands up in the air in frustration.

"Are you telling me that the great William Parker, fighter of demons, savior of the devout, fears Morty Spencer?"

"I'm not scared of anyone, well any human at least. But he makes people look like idiots, James. Who knows why he wants to talk to us or what dirt he thinks he has on us."

"You're priests, how bad could it possibly be?" Father Michaels asked.

"You are asking that with a serious face," James cut in saying. "It is tabloid television."

"Yes, it probably is boys, but do you know what the upside is to it?"

In unison, they both questioned, "Yes, please, what?"

"That our diocese thought two young, handsome priests would be better than an elderly priest."

"You aren't that old, what are you sixty-five?" James said, knowing exactly how old he was.

"You know very well that I'm only fifty years old Father Clapper, now don't try and raise my blood pressure, the doctor said I'm supposed to stay calm."

James laughed, and Billy said, "You picked the wrong business if you were looking for something stress-free."

"I didn't pick it; a woman came to me saying she had demons in her house and that they were scared to go home. Does that ring a bell, you haven't forgotten that, have you?"

"No, unfortunately, I can still see that like it was yesterday," Billy replied attempting to remain calm.

"So, you just want us to answer honestly, to be clear?" James asked.

"You're priests, why would you want to lie? Yes, just do your best to satisfy his questions. I'm more than sure that in a half hour we'll all be laughing about this sitting back at the church having dinner," Father Michaels tried to say in a manner where he could calm the two men's worries.

"You are taking us out to eat for doing this, you've got a church budget," Billy said smiling and adjusting his collar.

A light knock came at the door and someone with a headset poked their head in smiling. "Fathers, is there anything you need? You will be going on next if you could follow me, please. Father Michaels if you'd like to head up front we've reserved a seat for you. The boys said that you had issues climbing the stairs in your old age. I have a wheelchair here if you'd like it?"

Father Michaels shot daggers at the boys shaking his head. He smiled politely at the boys. "Father Parker, Father Clapper, break a leg out there. No, dear, I think that I will manage to make it all by myself. I thank you though, you are too kind."

The two followed the producer down a long hall busy with people running in and out of doors. James looked to Billy for any reassurance and he wasn't sure if he was going to pass out or be ill. "Would you pull it together, Billy, you look like you're going to puke your guts out, take a breath or something, would you?"

Billy gave a thumb up before sticking his head in a trash can and making just about the worst noise James had heard in a long time. "You are filling me with all kinds of confidence, Billy, are you going to be alright?"

He answered with a second round of puking and the producer started to look green in the face. "If he doesn't stop puking, I'm going to lose everything I've eaten today."

James smiled uneasily. "I'm sure he's-"

Billy did it again and the producer sprinted for a bathroom before an echo of puking came down the hallway. Everyone in the hall had stopped and was looking at the two priests, only James, of course, was able to see anything. He leaned over patting him on the back. "Are you going to be able to do this or not?"

Billy pulled his head out rising slowly testing his stomach to make sure he could sit up straight. When nothing tried to escape, he pulled a handkerchief from his back pocket, taking it across his chin he saw the bystanders. The producer came out of the bathroom and she did not look like she was overly pleased with him. He pulled out a second backup handkerchief and held it out for her. She shook her head, pointing to the door. "You don't want to be late, Fathers, Mr. Spencer is less than forgiving."

She opened the double set of steel doors. The two looked up, seeing a blinking green ON AIR sign. They came out to a smiling Morty Spencer standing and clapping as a large projection screen for commercial breaks raised itself off set and back onto the rafters above and out of view. Morty said, "Thanks again to our sponsors for the new soon to be a hit from comedian turned action star Bruce Willis in a riveting looking preview for Die Hard, what a movie that is going to be, make sure you catch it and if you're thirsty afterwards don't forget to get a refreshing Coors beer."

Billy leaned over to whisper to James. "I might need a beer when this thing is done. You think the big man would mind?"

"Please, you know that Father Michaels and the others take a finger of whiskey every so often. I'm sure that he'd forgive us. I'm sure he would pity us for being put through this in the first place."

"Remember that when I ask you to swing in and grab us some from the gas station after we get off the train."

Morty turned his attention to the two. "Would you please give up a round of applause for our local boys turned priests. They are Southside boys raised tried and true and have found God in their lives. Father Parker, Father Clapper will you please come, have a seat, and join me on the hot seat. We are very blessed, excuse the pun to have you here today. Welcome, come on don't be shy, come on folks these men will keep you from going to hell."

The crowd cheered holding up colorful signs and the two instantly wanted to melt and go back out to the safety of the busy hallway. James smiled uneasily looking at Billy. "I wish that I would have puked now too," James said.

"I told you, it's too late now," Billy said smiling.

"You didn't say anything, you said blah and then you did it again as you lost your very large breakfast in the garbage can outside," James said.

"If you'd have eaten as little as me growing up you would look forward to every meal you get."

The two took their seat on the guest couch. Morty had a smile from ear to ear. "Well, how are you doing today Fathers?"

"I've been less nervous in my life," Billy said with a smile no one would believe.

"Yes, Father Parker, I am quite sure that you are. Now are you referring to when you are out battling ghosts?" Morty asked with a knowing smile.

"Demons, Mr. Spencer, demons," Billy replied.

"Please, we are going to be old friends soon, call me Morty, call me Morty, let's try and be civil. Now you aren't Ghostbusters, just demon busters, is that what they call you?

"They call us priests, Morty," James said with a tinge of annoyance in his voice.

Morty was going full bore now and the crowd was whooping and hollering, "You ain't afraid of no ghosts, demons sorry demons, so how long have you two been fighting these demons?"

The crowd roared with laughter. James sat forward, taking long, deep breaths, trying to stay calm at the moment he wished this man was a demon so he could send him to hell where he belonged. But he was just a nuisance and there was very little that he could do to the man, he'd pledged an oath to God and the church and it was not one that he took lightly.

"We've been fighting demons for sixteen years," James said.

The crowd gasped whispering to one another. Spencer laughed, he loved his guests because up until now they'd all been just barely on the brink of being able to be referred to as sane. "You've been fighting them for sixteen years, I wish that I looked as young as you Fathers. You need to tell me what the secret is to your eternal youth. Is it one of the gifts bestowed upon you by God? Is there a God, do you have any insights into the man upstairs? Or are you trying to say you've been dealing with those dark things since you were ten?"

"We had an encounter when we were young, it was what started everything, it changed our lives...forever, Mr. Spencer," Billy said calmly and evenly as he leaned forward staring the man in the eye.

"Morty, remember we are friends, Father. The last one I want not on my side when the time comes is a priest of all things."

"We aren't friends yet, Mr. Spencer. I can't say that we probably will be. If you need to confess any sins, then maybe you could stop by the church." Billy replied.

Billy looked over to Father Michaels watching him as a courier was walking away and he was unwinding a string keeping an envelope closed. From there Billy could see the symbol that came on all their assignments.

Morty sat forward on his elbows, enthralled in the conversation and waiting for it to grow. He was waiting because he knew more than they gave him credit for. "Not friends, got it, so I can pull off the gloves and you aren't going to be too offended. Tell me how exactly does a ten-year-old send a demon back to hell? Did you use a Ouija Board, or something else?"

"We just assisted, Father Joseph and Michaels were the ones in charge. They did the heavy lifting."

"Who was this demon in, or what, I am biting my nails to know?"

"He'd possessed a four-year-old," James said with no nonsense just the facts.

"When you deal with these demons, the ones that have ascended from hell, how do you know that they are really demons? How do you know the person isn't just mentally ill? Do you really know that they are demons?"

"You have to be kidding me. Do you listen to your words; do you hear what you are saying aloud? Yes, we know that they are demons, we wouldn't do that to an innocent, it isn't our-"

"I'm sorry, James, you said, an innocent, please, what is that?"

"It's you, it's me, it is any human, anyone who is not possessed, not damned," Billy cut in as he was losing his patience.

"So, tell me...tell us, all of us, how do you know they've been taken? Do they fly around the room, do they spin their heads around in a circle, do snakes come out of their eyes?"

James looked to Father Michaels watching him walk off stage, envelope in hand and the crest on his letter all too familiar. He knew well that there was someone needing to be sent back to hell. "I believe that you have mythical confused with demons, Mr. Spencer. They can crawl up the wall, their eyes can glow, levitation is even possible, I have seen a four-year-old send a grown man up against the wall."

"That is fascinating Father Clapper. Do you mind if I call you James, it would feel so much more personal, do you mind?"

"Yes thanks, I do."

"You do what?"

"Mind, I know you don't believe us, you don't believe in demons, but I assure you I've had many things burnt into my soul that haunt me in my sleep."

"That's chilling, Father Parker, so four-year-olds, can we talk about those a little?"

Billy didn't like the question and was waiting for him to finish and move on to a new topic unknowing that would be the final subject today. "What can we answer for you about those, they typically don't possess them, however, it's happened to children more than once, unfortunately," Billy explained.

"Yes, but when you said that you started when you were ten years old, is that because your brother Tony had been taken, he'd become one of them? How is good old Tony nowadays? How is he doing, is he fighting demons as well or is he still possessed? Didn't he do a little stint in the nuthouse?"

Billy raised to his feet, as did James, holding out a hand to Morty squeezing it harder than a man of the cloth ought to but nonetheless shook keeping Billy from stepping any closer to the overzealous cocky talk show host. "Until we meet again, Mr. Spencer and thank you again for choosing us to be on the show."

Morty winced from the shake and stood to clap for the two priests as they walked off the set.

Billy and James walked back to their dressing room, hoping that Father Michaels had stopped there and had been patient enough to wait. They assumed it had been their assignment that had come in and both were more than ready and willing to take it on. Father Michaels was pacing back and forth, cigarette hanging from his lips, he tossed the pictures on a table. "He's back at it again, but this looks so much worse?"

"So much worse than what?" James asked nervously.

"Than seventy-three, eighty-one, or eighty-five," Father Michaels said as he plopped down on the visitors' couch. He looked up to the ceiling like he was praying silently.

"That's a lot worse than I thought you were going to say. Is it close, or do we need to jump on a plane?" Billy asked.

"It is your choice boys. You've been at this almost exactly as long as I have, except I have been guarded by God and been a member officially since the beginning. The two of you were dumped into this because we needed to rid the demon from your brother. God, please help us and deliver us from evil."

"Whoa, slow down Father, what do you mean we can get on a plane or we cannot get on a plane? You just named off every one of the worst things we've ever heard of at least in our time." James said as he tried his best to keep his tone civil, respectful, and not scream aloud.

"The reason I said it that way is because it is your choice. It is free will, something you forget that God bestowed upon you...upon everyone. You can go, you can stay, you can fight, or you can sit around and wait for hell to-"

"We aren't running. If there's a job that needs to be done, something here that needs to be accomplished, we are doing it here. We aren't running, we aren't hiding, we sure as hell aren't abandoning the people of this city!" Billy yelled as he slammed his hand down on the counter.

"Never thought the latter, son. Just read the file, let me know where you are at. They are coming back and we will have to see if they are after anyone we know."

Billy walked forward to him concerned. "Do you think they'd come back after Tony; I've never read that they've come after anyone twice before? Is there a chance that you guys didn't fully get rid of it, that not all of it was sent back to hell, is that possible, can that happen?" Billy said almost pleading.

"We might be going into uncharted waters boys. We can't say yes, we can't say no. We'll find out when we find out. You might want to swing in though, and see how your brother is doing. I'm sure that he is fine, but it won't hurt to see him anyway. Your mother doesn't get to see you often enough, trust me, all she does is ask about you, worry and ask about you."

"Mother's worry, it's what they do," Billy said.

"If you are doing the hometown job, then go for it, but go over and see how they are when you are finished. We only get the information after it's happened. If we can nip it in the bud, then we do. Good luck you two, may God be with you."

"He always is, put in a good word with Father Joseph next time you speak to him," James said.

"Will do boys, I'd say take it easy on them, but they went to hell for a reason too, go get those demons. You know you guys are the best I have," Michaels did the sign of the cross. He patted each of the boys on the shoulder as he walked out of the dressing room. The boys could hear the opening of his zippo as he walked out.

"You ready to go do this?" Billy asked already knowing James would rather give up his life, then let just one of those things stay on Earth.

James and Billy both opened their travel cases. Each had a state of the art video camera. The church had been directed by the Vatican as early as the technology had become available, to begin trying to record the exorcisms, for if they should ever need proof that they would have it. The church was beginning to see that those devout were growing fewer, belief in God was being questioned, and sins were not diminishing, if anything they were getting worse.

The fact that crack had hit the streets that year and then had exploded across the ghettos of America was disturbing. Those in the suburbs and the other high-end communities had not seen it coming because it had not affected the rich, white, well-off citizens. Not until a congressman's son had thought he was doing something totally different at a party and had overdosed and been found choking on his own vomit, it had gone almost unnoticed. It had made drug dealers more money than they could possibly store in a row of warehouses.

Billy and James picked what they needed to arm themselves with the tools that Michael had bestowed upon them as well as some innovations they had come up with on their own. They'd been thinking of ways to kill demons since they were ten, by the time they made it through seminary school and graduated to demon removal each had a notebook full of ideas. Father Michaels could only shake his head when he saw the ideas that they had come to him with early on. He'd never had a doubt about the two, but it only concreted it more.

Chapter 6

Parkes' Residence Chicago's Southside

Billy looked up at the two-story run-down house. It screamed ghetto and poor, and it felt like home. If they walked in and the father was sitting there lifeless to the world, and drunk at noon on a weekday he wouldn't be surprised. James snapped his fingers, bringing him back out of his daze. "You with me, Billy? I'm going to need you solid on this one, brother."

Billy blinked, backing up and brought up his fists. He took a deep breath when he saw his best friend and partner looking worried for him holding up his hands to try and block the punch. "You scared the hell out of me."

"You're welcome then," James said with a grin trying to ease things.

Billy opened his mouth to say something and then realized James was just being a good friend. "Bless you, smart ass. I didn't mean to go anywhere it was just the house, it reminds me of my mom's. I started thinking of Tony, and my dad, and it didn't bring back any good memories. We had plenty of good ones after he was gone, but nonetheless some of those run deep. It changed our lives...forever."

"It made your dad leave which I'd say was a blessing. You two probably would have had to kill him if it meant surviving the rest of your preteen years and twenties. That day was the worst one I can remember when your mom needed the hospital and the two of you had to stay across the street."

"That couple was great. Ralph treated us like we were his own kids over the years. He taught Tony and I how to drive."

"Yeah, and you still don't own a car," James said smiling.

"Who needs it with an L train at your beck and call. It was good for Tony, sent him down the path to be a mechanic, kept him out of trouble. I would've been okay if he didn't buy a bike, but he has a good head on his shoulders and he'll be okay. Besides, he has Alecia to keep him level headed until he gets into seminary school."

A voice cleared startling the two; neither had noticed the disheveled looking mother and father at the door. The mom instantly put all her faith into the two priest's arrival. "Are you here to help? Are you here to help our children?" The mother asked.

"Honey, don't put too much faith into this. This is for quacks, they need a doctor, we are wasting time."

Billy knew that there was always one skeptical parent. Usually the parent who was only going to church because of their spouse's religion. "Sir, ma'am, we are going to do everything in our power to save your child."

"Children," the woman said.

James held up a hand not wanting Billy to talk any longer. He could tell that he was already annoyed with the dad. The father had done nothing wrong, they'd had more people than they could believe who had been skeptical, even after seeing their children and loved ones possessed by those of the dark ways. "What do you mean children. The file just gave us the address."

"They don't even know what is going on. That's it, we are taking the kids to the hospital, now," he said as he stamped his foot in frustration.

"We can leave, Mr. Parkes, there's other places that need our help. We came here because you are Southee's and you look like better times are hopefully in your future, no offense," Billy said holding up his hands. "The reason you don't see this in the news is it is something that you don't want others to know about. No one is ever proud to say that his or her child had been possessed by a demon. My baby brother, who isn't so much a baby anymore had it happen, he almost died. We almost died, but we fought back, my mother got help and we got my brother back and sent the demon back to hell where it belongs."

When the man opened his mouth to say something the woman brought an elbow across into his gut. "Shut up, Dale, they are here to help. I called, they are going to help and if they save our children, then it is going to be the greatest thing we have ever gotten from the church. Just because you lost your way in the church doesn't mean that I have. Maybe this will help you find your way back."

The man bent down, grabbing at his gut. When Dale came back up he had an opened hand ready for his wife. Billy cleared his throat, "Dale, if you lay a hand on that woman you will have more than demons in your home to be concerned about, abusive fathers and husbands are not something the church sees as a good trait. You might think we are a bunch of quacks, but if you've seen what is in my head, then you'd be quiet and open that door with open and thankful arms."

Dale kept his hand up for a moment before he began to lower it. "My wife doesn't have anything to worry about; it's just that...I've never seen anything like this. Lorraine, if this doesn't work, then we take them to the hospital, do we have a deal?"

She nodded, giving him a hug. "Thank you, Dale, I know it sounds crazy, but I don't think that they are going to get help at a hospital. We tried taking them to the doctor and all they did was give them pills that didn't do anything, how they were saying something ignorant about vitamin deficiencies."

James walked up getting ready to go in. "You did say children, Mrs. Parkes?"

"Yes, Hayley and Martyn, they are twins," Mrs. Parkes said.

"How old?" Billy asked.

"Ten, why?"

"The Shining, great," James said as he walked up looking inside. "You stay out here, we'll go in and try and do what we can. Where are they?"

"We don't know, they ran up the stairs and disappeared earlier, after they threw Dale from about halfway up the stairs. I'd try going upstairs."

"We'll figure it out. You two stay here, please. Parents have a hard time dealing with things that we have to do to get their loved ones back," James said.

"What are you going to do?" Mr. Parkes questioned.

"Whatever it takes to send that demon back to hell," James said as he turned around and shut the door to the home turning the lock behind him.

Billy set down his briefcase pulling out a video camera with a wide angle lens and tripod placing the setup to it in the corner. James did the same and the two could hear laughing. The two of them were unsure where they were and the laughing only grew louder. Billy asked, "So does the fact that they are twins and hence there are two of them creep you out in the least?"

"I think the fact that they are laughing and we can't see them is what is creeping me out, James. The fact that the parents are outside of their own home not knowing what we are about to do to their children creeps me out. The fact that the Catholic Church wants us to video record this so that they can show other people creeps me out. I have a lot of things right now that are-"

"Creeping you out Billy?"

The girl came to the edge of the steps laughing. "Do you want to come and play with us; do you want to be our friend?"

"We'd love to talk to you, Hayley; can we talk to you please?"

"Hayley isn't here puppet. Go away now while you can. You will not have a choice if you stay here very much longer."

"Where is your brother, where is Martyn?"

She ran a nail down the side of her cheek, cutting it deep. Blood began to run down her face, she held her hand under it dipping her tongue in it before laughing hysterically. She placed a bloodied small hand onto the wall running it along the wall as she disappeared back into the bedrooms."

James walked to the windows and door running a line of salt across them, at this point these actions were second nature. Both knelt and the two of them smiled thinking of Father Michaels and how terrified they'd been when he took them on an exorcism of their own. It was the first time that they would be responsible for and would have the weight of the actions taken to set upon their shoulders. They did the sign of the cross, saying cavete daemones.

"Alright, Billy, do we go find both of them and we send them back to hell or do you want to do this one at a time like we are used to?"

"I have no idea, James; I'd like to think if we can get them separated, then maybe we can team up and take the last one out."

"Right, but is that going to work?" James asked.

Billy didn't answer until he began up the stairs. "We won't know until we get in there. We can learn, we can know what did and didn't work next time, but we won't know a thing if we don't get out there and get our feet wet. There might be a time where there are three, where there are four, imagine an entire outbreak of these, there's a lot of things that might happen, but there's no reason to quit and there is no reason to doubt in what we are able to do. We kick butt and take names."

"Solid plan," James said as he followed him up grabbing a few glass balls filled with holy water from a pouch.

Two shadows began to make their way around them moving impossibly fast. One began to mock them; it was impossible to know who it was for most demons' voices sounded the same. "Do you ants like spiders?"

The two were barely listening, they knew taunting was something they did and that it needed to be ignored or be driven insane. James whispered, "I hate spiders!"

"Ignore them, James, this isn't our first time," Billy said.

Billy stopped when he didn't hear James' footsteps going up behind him. He was plastered against the wall brushing at his arms frantically. Billy yelled, "What in God's name are you doing, James, what is wrong?"

"Spiders, spiders, there are thousands of them, everywhere on me. Get them off, get them off now!"

They'd tried, unsuccessfully, the demons that is, to get in the two priests heads before, but never like this. Billy wanted to help his friend, but truly was unsure what to do to help. He took one of his bottles of holy water, not wanting to throw glass balls at his best friend and pulled the cap showering where he was brushing most at his arms off. The spiders that only James could see melted away and James fell back against the wall, his chest rising and falling. He held up his hands, blinking and shaking them a few times before what he saw was gone.

"You good, James, they gone?"

"We erase that from the video later," James said quietly seeing the two red lights pointing in their direction from the tripods.

Billy started his walk back up the steps; this time the echoes of James followed him. When they got to the top of the steps the blonde-haired girl, Hayley was already at the end of the hallway disappearing into the back room. She walked not like a little girl, but a woman that worked the streets and knew what men wanted to see.

"These things are messed up," Billy said.

The boy came out shaking his head, "Leave, send in the breeders, we need more in our army. The two of you will never be worthy."

James took a ball of water and lobbed it down the worn wood floor. The ball hit the wall, shattering but the boy's feet came up off the floor missing the water. "You want to play? We can play."

Martyn pulled his arms into his sides and pushed them both out with hands outstretched. An invisible force came down the hall, sending frames off the wall, shattering to the ground before making contact with James and Billy. They both tried to jump out of the way, but whatever force he was using to power it was enough to send the two men off their feet and backwards.

The demon child floated forward after them almost as fast as they were falling down the stairs. It was screaming at the top of its lungs as they descended the hall and staircase. Both closed their eyes, waiting for the impact. When they realized they had not hit the hard floor they opened their eyes to see the demon floating above them. He raised his arms swinging the two in a circle and into a wall. The demon's laughter was all they could hear echoing throughout the home.

James threw a handful of holy water filled glass balls just to the side of them. When the water splashed off the walls the demon yelled words, they could only assume were not of the flattering nature.

He pulled James close to him until the demon's eyelashes were tickling his cheek. He pushed out sending James across the living room and through the large glass bay window. James hit hard against it. The glass broke beneath the force and the shattering glass went everywhere as he went through it. His foot went through the salt line he'd made. James could feel blood trickling down the back of his neck when he tried to sit up. He tried to shake it free from his brain, but only made the dizzy spells worse.

Dale and Lorraine just watched in awe. She tried to rush toward him, but Dale gripped her around the waist. "You aren't going anywhere, you just saw him fly out of our window, right?"

"Dale, he needs our help?" she protested.

"He needs someone's help but it sure as hell isn't ours. Christ, would you look at him, he flew twenty feet!"

Morty and his crew sat in the news van. The three all had their mouths agape. "Rod, Nick, if you two aren't getting this then you'll never work in this town again!"

"You're kidding, right; we were already watching the mom and dad on the porch. This is great, what made him do that, Morty, did you set something up with these quack jobs?" Rod asked.

"No way, I wish I had that kind of budget. I wanted to show the world they were frauds, not make them look like God's holy warriors. Oh my, would you look at that!" Morty practically yelled as he shook Rod by the shoulder.

"You want shaky footage or you want this to look like a pro shot it, Morty?"

"It's Mr. Spencer to you, Rod, and I'll like you to show me a little respect. You keep it steady and still, this is too good to pass up!"

The scene couldn't have been better for the devil's doing. The drapes were blowing in the wind, the clouds were dark, removing any sun from the day and a thunder in the distance began to shake the ground. "This is going to make the news, screw the show!" Nick said, bouncing up and down as he dialed in his equipment on the panel.

Morty spoke low into his microphone as if something might hear him. He said, "Folks, you are watching live recorded footage. We are following our guests from a show we did earlier today with catholic priests, Father Parker and Father Clapper. We followed them from our studio to the house here, which is the Parkes' residence, at least that is what the mailbox says. This is never before seen footage and Morty Spencer is bringing it to you first. We just got video of Father Clapper being thrown through the window, by what we don't know, but there is no need to worry, I can assure you for his well-being by the way he was tossed out. The chances of him not needing a doctor and hospital will be a miracle all in its own if....what are we doing sitting in the van?"

Morty didn't have to give the two directions if they wanted to keep their jobs. He swung the van door open and charged to the downed priest. James heard the door and for a minute thought that maybe demons were on the streets and chasing him. He saw Morty smiling from ear to ear sprinting toward him. James could tell if it were just the slightest bit windier that his horrible toupee would blow free and expose his hair, or lack thereof for all to see. A scream came from the house and brought him back to life. He was going to say something, but Hayley came up to the broken window laughing and floating in place.

When she saw her two parents, she smiled and rushed out the window. James was going by instinct only at this point. He rolled to his side getting up to a knee and then stumbling forward. He could hurt later he thought, God would give him no test that he was not able to handle.

He got some momentum just as she was within reaching distance of her parents, her arms outstretched toward them, the blood from earlier covering her face and her teeth exposed for everyone to see.

James ripped his belt off pulling it out of the loops clean and slid it back through the buckle. He took her by the back of her dress and tossed the loop over her head and shoulders, pulling it tight and never stopped moving back toward the house.

The demon screamed as loud as she could at the thought of her two fresh souls being pulled just out of her reach. James yanked hard behind him, sending her back into the house with him. He swung her in a circle, taking her by the shoulder and pushing her down by the chest to the ground. He pulled a plastic bag full of salt from his pocket still moving into the living room with the demon in tow. He used his teeth to tear open the bag, and held his hand beneath it catching a handful of it in his palm as the demon tried its best to get back out of the house. James pulled her back one more time and leapt forward throwing a handful of salt onto the windowsill recreating his protective barrier against the damned leaving.

He heard his belt fall to the ground and watched as she disappeared back up the steps laughing as she did. The fact he didn't see or hear Billy when he got his bearings back hit his sense of urgency all at once. "Billy, Billy, where are you, where are you?"

The voice he assumed was coming from Martyn echoed down the stairs, "We are going to sacrifice him to our dark lord if you do not come."

James was anything but ignorant. He knew it was a trick or to be accurate a trap. He started up the stairs trying to figure out how he was going to save his friend from not one but from two demons. He didn't like the odds and knew there wasn't anything that he could do to better them. By the time that he tried to get reinforcements here they would have the entire block under their mind control, or have passed from these youth's bodies to a new one.

A red light came from beneath the door. James did not waste time outside once he heard Billy's cries from the room. He kicked the door once, then twice and it did not budge. He threw one of the glass balls filled with holy water on the knob crashing it and breaking the glass. James ran back as far as he could against the wall and came for it practically doing a flying sidekick into it, he thought of Chuck Norris and realized the man would have a heart attack if he saw this poor excuse for martial arts he was attempting to perform. Nevertheless, his foot connected just to the side of the knob and this time when he hit it the door snapped along the edge. The door flung open and James looked around for Billy.

Billy had sweat and blood covering his face. The demons didn't usually waste their time with beating the non-possessed, but Billy must have been taunting them trying to buy time until James could come and do something. Billy saw James and tried to smile, but his cheek looked like he had a baseball in the side of it. The one taking over Martyn laughed when he saw the look of hope on Billy's face. "Your brother's face will not have the same hope that your face does when they go for him."

"What are you talking about, demon?" Billy yelled.

"We won't have to explain anything once you are one of us. Be patient priest," the demon holding Hayley screeched.

James looked for something to help him, the crosses on the wall were burnt to a char state. The only thing that was holding it up was a rusty nail. Martyn motioned with his hand and it wiggled loose from its spot. Hayley motioned to the other one as well as two from the wall boards and it did not take a genius to know what intentions they had for him or what his plans were. They pulled the nails toward him and had Billy up against the wall pinned, unable to move and making him out to look like Jesus on the cross. The two possessed spun their hands counterclockwise and Billy very quickly began to spin until his head was down and feet up. "Our father will love this gift. You priests are truly a treat for him. We will deliver you to evil, be patient and soon you will see why he is not your God and is the one to truly fear."

The first nail was pressing into his hand; the first drop of blood began to make its way from his palm. James tossed a handful of glass into the air as Hayley held up a hand keeping them suspended and with her free hand brought James off his feet. She sent him flying backwards until he slammed against the wall behind him twice, and then brought him slowly toward her. His feet dragged on the wood floor as she brought him toward her. She squeezed her other hand, making the glass balls break open and fall to the floor. Martyn's demon yelled, "Be careful with those, what are you thinking?"

"Shut up, for you know nothing of what you say!" She pulled James in even closer, laughing and brought out a blackened tongue, bringing it up from his cheek to his temple. His skin sizzled as whatever power she had burned as her tongue made its way up his face. James could hold it no longer and when she saw the smile on his face after getting the burn realized something was wrong. He flexed his wrist breaking the holy water ball that was under his watchband and giving him control of it again.

Most people want to make the demons get as far away from them as possible but not Father James Clapper. He gripped onto her dirty and torn dress holding on tight and pulled her in closer to him. He released the holy water he'd taken a drink of, and had been holding in his mouth. It sprayed across her face, the veil of evil slowly came away and he slammed her to the ground. He dragged her by her hair to the old heater slamming her against it and brought his belt one last time he hoped around her neck and stuck her to the pipes pulling as tight as he could until there was no slack left to be given.

Martyn's demon screamed and seemed to forget all about Billy letting him collapse to the ground. He looked behind him and screamed, "Stay, you little ant of God, we aren't done with you yet."

Billy watched in horror as the first nail finished making its way into his hand. He poked around in his pocket with his right hand wishing he had something...anything that he could use. He was trying to think of what to do, but could come up with nothing. He pulled his rosary beads from his neck, throwing them onto the demon. They hit him like a brick sending him to the floor just shy of Hayley's feet. Billy pulled his hand free screaming as the nail tore the rest of the way through his hand. He leapt onto the boy flipping him over, pulling his Bible holding it to Martyn's head and the two began screaming as loud as they could, the blood from his hand covering the demon's face. Billy said, "My Lord, you are all powerful, you are God, you are Father. We beg you through the intercession and help of the archangels Michael, Raphael, and Gabriel, for the deliverance of our brothers and sisters who are enslaved by the evil one. All saints of Heaven, come to our aid. My Lord, you are all powerful, you are God, you are Father. We beg you through the intercession and help of the archangels Michael, Raphael, and Gabriel, for the deliverance of our brothers and sisters who are enslaved by the evil one. All saints of Heaven, come to our aid."

Hayley was screaming and thrashing to get loose. The thought of the two sending them back to hell made her want to tear their heads off...literally. Martyn began coughing as the demon left his body. His color began to come back and his body convulsed as the final hints of the demon left his body. Billy and James wasted no time turning their attention to the demon possessing Hayley. "Get away from me, you will not make me fail, you will do nothing by the time you think you've accomplished something, he will have taken more lives than your small mind can fathom!"

The two looked at each other trying to imagine who she was talking about, but not taking very long for either of them to conclude that it was Satan and he was making another play at Earth, a serious one this time.

"Hayley, Hayley, what is wrong with you, why do you look like that?" Martyn said, tears were filling his eyes, unable to mentally accept what he was seeing, and the sound coming from his sweet, young sister.

Her voice changed back to normal for only seconds, "Come here sweet, Martyn, come to me."

He crawled quickly past the two priests before they could catch the small boy. Her eyes went back to their natural, unpossessed color of almond. When Martyn got within reaching distance of her, she took hold of his arm and leg and even from her angle tied to the radiator heaved the boy with no care of his well-being. "If you aren't one of us then you can die just like the rest!"

Martyn was instantly up in the air and the window shattered when his small fame struck it. Martyn screamed as he disappeared from sight. James passed over the demon kicking it in the face as he leapt out the window with no care for his own personal safety. He landed on the awning outside their window. Martyn was dangling on the edge and his fingers were beginning to slip down the shingled space that was saving his young life. James took his hand seconds before he let go, he could see Morty pointing at the house with the news camera directly at him. James could just see the talk they were going to have with Father Michaels if they made it out of this alive.

Screams from a new body came and this time was from their mother Lorraine. "Is that you, Martyn, are you okay baby?"

Dale pushed her out of the way running out beneath the awning. "Is he okay, Father?"

"He won't be if you don't catch him! I can't hold him much longer!"

James looked to his hand, it was wet with perspiration and the boy's chubby fingers were slowly sliding from his grasp.

"Drop him, I got him, I'll catch him!"

James opened his grasp on the boy letting him fall. He screamed, but it subsided instantly when his dad caught him with both arms and the two collapsed onto the ground. His mother leapt down the stoop to them, stealing the boy from Dale and hugging him until he squealed. The boy couldn't control the tears and the mother wasn't doing much better. Morty said, "What is it in there, Father Clapper, what is it in there?"

James ignored him completely. "Dale, get that boy across the street and away from here, somewhere safe! Take Lorraine with you!"

Billy screamed for help and James quit talking, spinning and jumping up gripping the broken glass, ignoring the pain, grunting and pulling himself up. The shards of glass tore through where his fingers and hands attached. He swung his foot getting momentum and bringing an arm up. His suit coat acted as a barrier protecting him from the glass. Hayley was standing over Billy, who was holding his Bible in one hand. The other had a cross with blood dripping from his hand. The leather belt that had been holding her to the heater was ripped and on the floor at her feet.

James threw the glass balls of holy water at her feet; they shattered and smoke began to rise from her toes. The holy water made her levitate instantly and James ran leaping and wrapping his arms around her neck. The two of them flew across the room, crashing into the wall. "Let go of me you stupid puppet!"

James did not comply and the two proceeded to knock off the shelves and knickknacks from the wall and dresser when they collided into it. Billy rushed the two of them wrapping his bloodied hands around her left arm. James let go taking her right and the two both took holy water and dumped the small vials of it over her head. She screamed and finally stopped levitating falling to her knees. The two recited the same prayer as before to save her soul as well as her life. She thrashed, kicked and did everything in her power to try to free herself, but they had her now, dead to rights.

The two cameramen watched nervously as Morty walked closer and closer to the door while the screams echoed down the street. By now the entire neighborhood had begun populating their stoops. Dale yelled, "Get back in your homes, it isn't safe!"

They stood there dumbfounded trying to see what was going on, the two floors both now had broken windows, the curtains flapped in the wind and a bloody, beaten looking Martyn was curled into his mother's protective arms clutching her neck. She was doing the best that she could to soothe the boy, but it was doing little good.

Morty started walking toward the door. He looked behind him, Rod and Nick both tried to weigh what it was that they were doing and if it was worth it. "If the two of you don't follow me into that house, then you can walk home. Not sure you want to go and do that in this neighborhood."

They followed him, neither happy about it, but after the crash of the economy in the eighties the last thing either of them wanted to do was be unemployed, especially in their forties. Morty held up a hand before getting the countdown from Rod to start. "The two of you do anything to screw this up, you are gone. This is solid gold and we...I mean no I do mean that, I am going to skyrocket like never before after this. Everyone in the world is going to want to air this footage and it is going to make me a legend. Now count me in!"

Rod pointed behind him, Morty heard the footsteps and went to run, but Dale, who did not have a child clinging onto his neck sprinted.

"Hayley, Hayley, baby, are you okay, are you okay?"

The only thing that could be heard were her cries. James took the steps slowly; his back and knees were feeling the day after the window. She had bloody handprints on the back of her worn flower print dress from the cuts he'd endured when he had to jump back up from the awning. Dale hugged James and Hayley at the same time. She winced, jumping and let go of James and wrapped her arms around Dale's neck.

James got up close to his ear. "You need to take them to the hospital Dale, you need to take the family there, get the kids looked at, please."

"I thought you got the demons out of them, you sent them to hell where they belong, right?"

"I did, but that doesn't mean they are healthy. People who have been possessed can be severely dehydrated, worn down, muscle fatigue, on the brink of starv-"

"For the love of God, never mind, I'll take them, there's nothing more important than family. I can see that now. How can we ever repay you? Where is the other priest, is he okay, did something happen to him?"

Billy walked down the steps. He had his hand up against his stomach holding it with his good arm. "I'm going to be alright, I took a nail in my hand."

"Do I want to ask how?"

"Your possessed son thought it'd be a good idea to crucify me upside down in his bedroom. When they almost took Father Clapper out I had to rip my hand free to stop him. If we got him back, then it is all worth it."

Dale patted Billy on the shoulder. "You two have a place at my table anytime you need it, you just stop by, no need to call, we'll be here with open arms."

Lorraine was barely able to hold it together. She walked over with a quivering lip as she tried to say thank you to the two of them. She gave Billy a hug and moved to James and repeated it.

Morty swung in his microphone. "Mr. Parkes, Mrs. Parkes, can I ask you a question, please, Hayley, Martyn, can I please ask you a few questions? Did you see hell, did the devil welcome you with open arms?"

Dale raised a fist toward Morty. "You hit me and I'll be adding just one more property to my list, Mr. Parkes."

Dale brought his fist back, but James slipped in between them. "He isn't worth it, I'm sure it would feel wonderful, but it isn't worth it, I am confident, very confident."

Morty said, "I take that personally, Father Clapper. You are supposed to be a man of God; what kind of a way is that to act?"

"Me being a man of God and you acting the way you are is the only thing saving you from looking up at us from the ground."

Morty took a few steps back, holding his hand up. "I'm a lover not a fighter."

Nick laughed, trying to keep the camera steady and Morty shot him a glance only losing his cool persona for a second. "You owe the Father; you think this place is something I'm worried about losing then you are sadly mistaken. We aren't stepping foot back in this place if you dropped a tanker of holy water on it." Dale said.

Dale shook hands again with James and Billy before heading to his work truck where they all climbed in getting ready for the trip to the hospital and the first of hopefully many days of happiness and demon free living. They wasted no time getting in and headed out.

James looked to Billy once they'd left. "How are you doing, we need to get you to a hospital."

Billy shrugged, "I've been better. I'm not going to a hospital though, no time for it."

"You are aware that you have a hole...through your hand, right? You didn't get hit too hard on the head that you forgot that?"

"No, believe me, I am perfectly aware of the fact that I have a new hole in my body that I didn't have when I woke up. I don't think we have a lot of options. I can take care of my hand later."

"How long does it take for a doctor to put a couple stitches in it and give you a quick tetanus shot? You really don't think we can do that?"

"James," he looked over seeing Morty and his crew watching him and tried to regain his composure. "Father Clapper, did you hear them when they spoke, do you remember what they said? They are going after my brother, that or they are trying to trick us. I don't think this day is over, and I don't think wasting time sitting in a hospital while they take over more souls than we can count is a good idea. I only need one hand to do the sign of the cross."

"Right, but two sure does come in handy when there is a demon that needs to be held down," James said. "Come on we'll swing in, stitch you, and we will go, simple as that."

Morty cleared his throat, sliding over and giving the million-dollar car salesman smile. "I notice the two of you are in need of a ride, maybe my crew and I could be of assistance. Our life is to serve the-"

"Stop before my ears bleed, Mr. Spencer," Billy said, leaving him behind and heading to the van.

Morty did a fist bump watching as the two priests walked to the van. He looked around at the block. The neighbors, mostly wives who were caretakers for their children sat out front watching the two priests. They were holding rosaries in their hands and it was not hard to tell they were praying to the Man above.

Billy slid the door open to the van. Billy patted James on the back as he entered and then whispered, "Enjoy your interview, Father Clapper."

James turned around to see him stepping to the side and taking the passenger's front seat. He sat down, shaking his head thinking of a few things he would happily be telling him later. Rod took the wheel looking at Billy and his hand. He shook his head in disbelief. Billy said,

"Something on your mind, sir?"

"Rod, my name is Rod...I can't get my hands to stop shaking, I've never seen anything like that before...ever."

"Real stressful was it...watching us taking care of the demons, being thrown out of the windows, taken upstairs by force, having my hand nailed to the wall. You think you'll be okay, Rod?"

Rod opened his mouth to say something, but he realized there wasn't much he could say. He pulled out a box from beneath the seat offering it to a thankful Billy. He opened it with his good hand, looking at the contents. He gritted his teeth as he drained a bottle of disinfectant over his hand.

It bubbled and turned Rod's stomach at the thought of what he was feeling. Billy sat back in his seat, letting it air dry for a second and letting the pain subside for a moment before moving on to wrapping it with a few Band-Aids and covering that with a roll of ace bandages. When he was good Billy nodded and he started driving. Nick got up close to the window opening it and hanging the camera out to see the mass of people that had gathered in the street by now. "It's kind of a miracle," he said. "I mean, think about people and hope nowadays, this is amazing."

Rod said, "I still can't believe that you guys do this and no one knows about it. I mean the only people that we get on the show are absolute quacks, people who don't know what they are doing and more than likely have never seen a demon let alone dealt with one. I don't understand how you keep it so quiet."

Morty was going to tell the two of them to shut up, so he could begin interviewing James but Billy started replying. "Those that want attention for it typically are just witch hunters. They don't know what they are doing. Their training came from a book by someone who didn't know what they were doing either. James and I aren't here to get rich, between the two of us, we make less than twenty grand a year. If we had to repay our student loans we would be poor. We don't go around telling people about what we do. We aren't trying to stir the waters and bring the devil to town. Things like possession get glamorized, people, the innocents tend to forget how dangerous they are and that it can lead to death. There are no guarantees, we pray that when we rid someone that they will be okay, the long-term damage won't be something that is evident forever. We've seen people who have clawed almost all the skin from their faces trying to get the demons out of them, or they've been fighting them from taking over. They are scarred with that for the remainder of their lives. Their people understood what it means to be saved. If you were a devout member you would as well, and you wouldn't want to brag that the devil tried to take your loved one. Does that make sense, Rod?"

Rod was nodding slowly, he felt closer to God than a childhood of Sunday school had. Morty cleared his throat and a thin long microphone appeared to the side of Billy's face. "You know, just for the people at home, Father Parker, do you think there is any chance that maybe you could say that again into the microphone. I don't know how much of it I was able to pick up."

"No, there's not really a good chance of me repeating it, Mr. Spencer. Rod, you go north eight blocks and turn on Spielman Drive, take that three blocks to Bryant Lane, and don't stop until you hit Schmidt Avenue. You got that?"

"Not really, I'll just go straight and you tell me where to turn, you think that you could do that?"

James patted him on the shoulder. "Looks like that microphone doesn't really care if you sat up front does it, Father Parker?"

Billy held his hand now bandaged and could feel throbbing coming from beneath it. He knew that between Father Michaels and the lucky doctor who would be working on him he was going to get the fifth degree at some point. He smiled, watching the people passing by, each of them was saying thank you and he was nodding doing the sign of the cross for those giving him eye contact for as many people as he could.

Morty sat back realizing he couldn't get blood from a rock, and Billy was a rock if he had ever seen one. "Father Clapper, is there any chance that I could ask you a few questions please?"

"Knock yourself out, Mr. Spencer, but your questions end when we get to our location."

Billy said, "You can drop him off first, we don't need to drive in circles all day."

Rod, who didn't need to be told to let off the gas and they could all feel the van slowing down. Morty smiled uneasily for a moment before counting himself back in. "We are here on the mean streets of the Southside of Chicago and we have our esteemed guests from earlier. Now please let me just apologize, yes you heard me right, I need to apologize from the bottom of my heart. I didn't believe that what you did was real. Now I need to apologize again, because I have questions, oh lord do I have questions now!"

"You know we can't necessarily answer everything. We have secrets and we keep those so that we can keep that power to save people. There's nothing stopping a demon or Satan from watching your show, nothing keeping them from learning. They are older than time in some cases, you aren't aware of how intelligent they can be. The fact that he sent two into one house really says something."

"How did you know they were possessed and the mother wasn't just a little crazy?"

"Well, Mr. Spencer, they were flying, not like what you've seen in a Superman movie, but more like what you've seen when they go up a few inches near the window."

"Yes, and you pulled Hayley back in, is there a reason for that? What would happen if you would have let her stay out of the home, what could she do?"

"Every demon is different, Mr. Spencer."

"Please with the formalities, call me Morty, we are going to be good old friends one day sitting around my giant mansion enjoying drinks and talking about the day we met. I owe you two everything."

"We weren't really trying to get you famous, you realize we were doing our job, you were simply intruding on our day. I know we can't stop you from going forth with making it public, but you won't only catch the attention of the church, but you very well might catch the attention of others. Satan isn't flamboyant, and his demons try taking family by family, it is our job to save them before it is too late. We can't go around screaming to keep an eye out for demons, no one knows what to look for until it is too late," James said.

Billy pointed to the street sign, "Turn right there, drop off Father Clapper first."

As they approached the church Morty said, "Father Clapper before we drop you off, is there anything, anything at all you can tell the people at home?"

"Just that everyone needs to keep the faith. It won't completely protect them, but it can't hurt. The demons pray on the weak, or those with disabilities, they think they will get further going into those that people already try not to see the way it is in society. That if they can get so far in that they can get the others in their family, but when they start going after everyday children it means that the demons are coming out and they are doing it fast. They aren't trying to keep things quiet, they are going to go after something bigger."

Morty wasn't sure what to say, he nodded slowly thinking about it. "You mean there's more places in Chicago that are going to be under attack?"

"Not just Chicago," James said.

"America?"

James ran his hands through his hair. He couldn't believe this was happening on this scale, again. "Heaven."

Morty smiled nervously, he didn't know what to say. "Heaven? How in the hell, excuse my language, does he get into Heaven? I thought he was bound to hell?"

Billy spun around in his seat, smiling from ear to ear. "Really throws you for a loop the first time you hear a bunch of stuff for the first time, doesn't it? You want an interview, but I can confidently say you aren't quite ready to have it yet. You see if you can survive through this first session of possession. We are going to try and save as many people as we can, but if they go after anyone that we can't claim as church members the chances of us knowing about it are going to be quite slim."

James looked to Billy, "You always have such a poetic way with words, Father Parker. You sure you don't want me to come and talk to Tony with you?"

"No, not so long as our new friend and believer, Morty here decides to behave himself and really leaves when he drops me off there."

Morty held up his two fingers like a boy scout. "You've got my word. I should ask though; you boys or men are both quite young. How long does the church expect you to do what it is you do? I mean there can't be thousands of you out there doing such a thing, right? When do you get peace, I can't imagine dealing with these things daily."

"It isn't daily," Billy responded. "They aren't always here, not at least all the time I mean. But as far as how long we do it, I don't know. We took our vows much like someone vows to a wife, until we die and we are laid to rest. There's nothing that will keep us from doing what we need to do so long as it helps the church. My biggest concern is that we will be called upon and there will be a time that we aren't able to do anything to help, or worse that we will try and fail and have to watch the demons as they take the innocent."

"Is there a reason you two don't make more than twenty grand a year?" Morty said somberly.

Billy stared directly into the camera. "Because like I said earlier, we aren't in this for the money, the fame, and the notoriety. It is about

God and that is it. James I'll see you soon, please get Father Michaels up to date and tell him I'll be right back after I check on Tony."

James opened the door and slid out, shutting it hard enough to shake the van. Billy watched him until he disappeared inside of the church. He instantly felt alone and hoped that they'd not encounter anything along their travels to the garage. With his good hand, he patted his pocket, pulling out a few emergency placed holy water balls. Morty asked, "Can I ask what that is?"

"Holy water, we had them made. They work so well the church hired a glass blower just for creating these. We get fresh batches often enough. The last thing you want to do is be without holy water or your Bible. A few good prayers don't hurt either."

Rod started driving again looking around at the desolate streets, most homes needed repairs, most cars looked like they'd been sitting there for a while. When they pulled up to the garage Billy said, "If I were you I would get back to your news station and think long and hard if you truly want to get the devil's eye on you? Usually once you do, there's not a lot that you can do to get it back off you again."

He didn't give time for Morty or the others to answer.

Rod spun around into the back seat when he was far enough away that he didn't need to worry about Billy hearing him. "Morty, for the love of God, can we please, please, please go back to the news station. I don't think I want to be out here ever again. I might have to apply for a desk job, I am getting way too old for this crap."

"You don't want a Pulitzer?" Morty asked nonchalantly.

"Morty, I do, and you know that, but I like to think that our lives are worth more than a stupid award. I know they are a big deal, but I just can't imagine dealing with one of those things face to face."

"Hang in there, it sounds like it won't matter if you are in it or not. If there's a war going on, what better thing than a front seat for it?" Morty said.

"I think I agree with Rod, Morty, I don't want to have to deal with it either. Nothing would make me happier than fame, and money…at least what's left over after you take your good share and credit for anything."

"Watch it, there's a lot of men, young and old that would be happy to take your job."

"Really, well at the risk of the devil, I think that they can have it. You make sure to tell those men what they are getting themselves into by going that route if you think firing me to find out what is going on would deter them."

"You know what, you two are both ungrateful. Get us back to the studio, this is ridiculous."

Rod did as told driving a few feet before looking around trying to figure out where to go. He scratched at the dark stubble. "Either of you know where to go?"

Morty pointed forward and a detour sign was set up in the road. A construction worker with a stop sign pointed for them to go right. Rod gave him a thumb up as he rolled up looking at his options and seeing that he really had none.

Chapter 7

Billy waited for them to leave before he entered. He walked into a waiting room, seeing three women sitting in there and a few children by each of their feet smashing Hot Wheels together. "Good day, ladies, is there anyone around here that works?"

"They are all in the shop working. Every time we go in there to ask them when our cars are going to be done they just say twenty more minutes. I swear though every time they hear those doors open we see them running back to our cars."

He nodded, turning around, he was surprised when he opened the door, true to the lady's word they were hard at work. Billy walked around looking at the cardboard table in the corner. Each of them had a wrench in their hand and were standing around looking at an engine. "Hey, Mr. Holt, how are you doing today?"

"Oh hey, Father Parker, what are you doing here? You got one of the church's cars that needs to be worked on. We can put it up on the lift today for you. Anything to stay holy with the church, Father. Your brother ain't here, he had an appointment or something. I figured he would have been back by now though."

Billy gave a thumb up. He put a hand around the handle to leave when a wrench as long as his arm missed his face by mere inches. The glass exploded from the door's chain linked window, it only had him to come back toward. Billy shielded his eyes not having any death wishes or need for any other scars on his face from a demon's backlash.

Billy looked back to confirm what he was pretty sure he already knew and saw Holt staring directly at him smiling and already reaching for another wrench. His son put a hand on his shoulder and he brought the wrench around dead square in his jaw. The boy's head snapped to the side. Lenny tried to grip for the truck they were working on but passed out from the hit before his muscles could tell his hands to hold onto it. He fell into a clump on the ground where he lay and did not move again.

Holt's other son Garth wanted to run for his brother, but this man that had done that was not his father. He knew his dad to be tough and short tempered, but never, not once had he ever seen such violence from the man. "Dad, dad, what's wrong with you?"

Billy yelled, "You need to get out of here, Garth, you need to do it now, there's something very wrong with your father!"

Garth turned to run, but made it only a mere two feet before stopping. Billy could see it in his body language and knew that he was one of them now, there were two. He opened the door to the lobby ready to lock them in. The three women and their small horde of children were looking at him as he stood in the doorway.

Their eyes all glowed red, and their teeth looked pointed. The two women rushed toward his exit path, but Billy ran with all he could muster tackling the two before the demon's full power had taken effect. They yelled as he hit them hard enough to send them off balance. One of the pudgy possessed three-year old's jumped on him clinging to his leg. It tried to hold on tight, but Billy shook it off sending it into a pop machine.

He hated leaving this behind, but it was more than he could currently handle. He pulled the ax off the wall next to the fire extinguisher as he left and pushed out the door. He pulled it shut, letting it slam behind him. The demons who were giving chase slammed into the door. Billy put his shoulder into the door, keeping them from escaping the building. They screamed and moaned on the other side, taunting him as well. Billy looked at the ax and in-between slams into the door stuck it between the handle and the wall securing it tight enough that they couldn't break through.

The door slammed again and screeching came from the other side. Billy leaned his head against the door, patting the sturdy steel. Thud after thud continued until it went quiet. Billy ran down the street and around the corner to run through the alley.

Chapter 8

Morty and crew

Rod pulled around after the man directed traffic. "I only know how to get back to the station going the other way, Mr. Spencer. This isn't my normal route regardless of where I am. The Southside has never been real big on my list of places to hang out. I mean there was this one time with this girl Clara, holy hell, you should have seen this chick's rack, it was enough to bring a tear to-"

"Would you possibly please shut up, Rod," Morty barked. "I don't have the patience for this. We can't be late getting back, I want to start a bidding war among the news stations, and I'm not talking about local, I want to hit everyone up we've ever spoken to. We give them a picture that is clear, in focus, and steady of a little girl flying, a priest being taken upstairs, another one leaping out of a window to save a formerly possessed kid and I'm set, goodbye Chicago. I'll be on to bigger and better places galore."

"You mean, we'll be on to bigger and better places, right, Morty?" Nick asked.

"No, I'm pretty sure I said it perfectly accurate the first time, Nick."

Nick held the camera on his lap, his finger resting gently on the delete tape button. "You know once in a while it isn't a bad thing to not treat your crew like scum. You do realize that I got the video, all you did was have us be creepy and follow two priests whom you about made violent earlier. We remove this tape and you lose everything. I'm not an asshole, but far be it from me to let someone take my work, get the world handed to them on a platter and leave Rod and I in the ghetto because of it."

Morty went to say something, but saw Rod was watching them in the rearview instead of the road in front of them and yelled to the man. "Rod, you need to watch out for those...those...what are those?"

Rod instinctively hit his brakes almost losing control of the van. The rear wheel drive locked up and they skidded to a stop. Morty pushed Nick out of the way, pulling the camera out of his grip. The last thing he wanted him to do was something stupid and losing all of that golden footage. "What in the hell is going on, Rod? What is that going on up there? There must be a few hundred people out in the street. Is there a riot or a strike going on?" Morty inquired.

"Not that I know of. I haven't really had a chance to check, I've been recording shows for you all day and sitting in this stupid van the rest of my day," Rod explained.

"Just get through here without hurting someone. The last thing we need is to get sued for us running over some poor sucker," Morty said.

Rod tried to slow down, but when he saw what it was in the streets, he half debated punching the pedal and letting things fall into place the way that they did. The people walking the streets made him do a double take. He thought about them, thinking their eyes had been sunken in until he realized that wasn't the case whatsoever. These men and women were in their nicest clothes, but their eyes were either completely gone or hanging out of their sockets by what dry ligaments remained. "What is wrong with those people?"

Nick didn't take the question correctly and slid open the van's door. The two of them in unison, both screamed, "Don't open that door!"

The sound coming from the back was of it sliding open. Nick spun around to tell them sorry, unsure what he was supposed to do to help when eight hands reached in gripping his leather jacket and pulling him out of the van headfirst. The group that had pulled him out of there began gripping onto his clothes even tighter. When he fell out of the van his weight took them over. The fact that they were dead took little time to figure out. "Let go of me, let go of me...help...help me...help!!!"

One of the dead who was holding the sides of his jacket would have been close enough to kiss said through a dusty voice, "You will go nowhere, none of you will."

"You are dead, you are dead, how are you...how are you doing this, how is any of this possible?"

"The bones are dead, but the death that roams them is very much active."

Nick pulled back an arm to punch it in the face, unsure what it would do, but refused to sit still and let them do whatever it was they had intentions to do. An arm took his wrist not bothering to pull his sleeve back and clenched onto his wrist with all that it had.

The old teeth that had been below ground for a hundred plus years were like rocks. They ripped through his coat and continued until blood wetted its lips. Nick thought that it was the worst pain he had ever felt until another set of teeth came down on his index and middle finger biting until it came off.

He looked over his shoulder at his hand, seeing the blood squirting from his index and gushing from his middle. Tears filled his eyes and he screamed at the top of his lungs. He looked in astonishment at Morty hanging out of the sliding door and not to his amazement, holding the video camera smiling the entire time. Nick could hear him screaming for Rod. "This is gold, this is absolute gold, we got zombies, we got zombies in Chicago!"

Nick, who wasn't as impressed with the situation at hand tried to look around, but there was a pulling and all he could see was legs. A pair of teeth bit down on his cheek and another on the back of his head, his ear, and his nose. He tried to pull himself free but it didn't matter which way he tried to move there was pain.

Fresh tears made their way down his face as he screamed for all he was worth for help but his cries only fell on the ears of the dead. Crows sat in the tree cawing at them flapping their wings waiting for the leftovers should they come. When the dead had nothing left to pull from they started making their way to the street. They walked with a purpose chewing on the pieces of Nick that only fell down their neck and out in between their decayed ribs.

The birds circled around the bones in the street. Rod pulled Morty in by his collar. He lost his balance rolling over in the seat. Rod swerved the van pulling the wheel back to the side. "I got it, Morty, I got it, just a little bit longer and we will be good to go. It is an open street ahead of us."

The crows began to dive into the window. Their skulls smashed on the glass, blood and brains smearing and blocking his vision. Rod jumped, jerking the wheel, but still trying to keep it steady. A thousand crows took their turn crushing their skulls into the glass. Rod turned the wipers on but it only smeared the blood. "Slow down, Rod, what are you doing, you are going to crash the-"

The van hit the curb going up at first and then down. Morty flew into the rear, gripping Rod's shoulder, but losing it just as fast as he'd had it. Rod turned not thinking about it as he watched his boss and his dress shoes disappearing as he got near the edge of the door. Morty clung to the door with his manicured hands. Had Rod been able to see what was ahead of him, he would have done a hundred things differently.

The first would have been not driving directly into a hundred-year-old oak tree. When the van struck, the sliding door slammed shut with such force that it broke Morty's spine, nearly cutting him in half. A metallic taste instantly filled his mouth and he spat seeing nothing but blood on the ground beneath him. His toupee hung down in front of his face. He tried to push up from the ground half in, half out and screamed in agony.

He pulled himself half way out yelling for help. Morty tried to shake his head to get his hair piece out of his line of sight. He could just barely see through it, but temporarily felt relieved when he could see feet. In all the delirium of what was happening, he forgot who the owner of the feet belonged to. He tried to rush away, but he'd do nothing fast, but die.

The dead were unable to bend to reach him, one walked over him tripping into the van reaching for the camera and taking it away as it had been directed. The rest fell atop of Morty, dry tongues licked at the fresh blood on his scalp and chin.

Morty screamed for Rod, but no help was coming for him, he cried from the pain but again nothing was there. The crows were no longer cawing, they all were dead. He looked up to the sky becoming a believer in God instantly and hoping that there was one and that he was watching out for him. He tried to think of the sins he'd committed over the years, the laws he'd broken, the privacy of others that he had invaded and a thousand more things atop of that. By the time he was done running through the list, the first of the dead had fallen on him and was biting into his suit coat. Morty yelled, trying to push them off, but for every one of them he was able to fight back five more took its place.

Rod watched Morty in horror. He wanted to pull him back in but wouldn't stop the van for anyone or thing. He was not going to die because of this lesser human telling him what to do. He'd said it repeatedly how if they didn't take some of his power away at the television station that he was going to get someone killed. He tried to look for something to reach him, but with the look on the man's face that made him turn around. The view in front of his was blood soaked and the wipers would do nothing. Rod put his foot to the brake finally ready to give in but it was too late.

The van crashed into the tree doing upwards of thirty or forty miles per hour. Rod didn't have time to think about it and wasn't prepared. He tried to brace himself as he heard the crunch, but it happened too quick for anything worthwhile to be planned. Rod flew through the windshield, the glass broke tearing the sides of his face, his arms, and back. He thought his neck was broken but was unsure. He lifted his neck answering that question.

He tried to look around, but all he could see was blood pouring down his face. He screamed for help but they were in a desolate run-down part of town and not many went through it except to get to a different place. Tears began to make their way down his face. When he could finally see something, a horde was almost upon him, trying to reach him, but he was out far enough for making it unable for them to grasp ahold of him because of the rigor mortis in their bones.

Rod smiled, feeling a sigh of relief. He tried to say something to let them know that he would not be a meal, but his jaw didn't react when he tried to speak. He thought quickly it was broken, but it was better than what happened to the other two. He didn't know what to do, but figured if he didn't bleed out he would have the time that he needed to figure it out. A clicking sound came from behind him. He couldn't turn his head to see what was going on but when the first set of teeth bit into his calf, then his thigh and his butt, he lost track. The lights started to dim, but not before one final bite clenched deep into his neck and pulled hard enough to pull a strip of skin from his neck to the middle of his back, it was the worst pain he'd ever felt just before he passed and joined Morty and Nick.

Chapter 9

Holt's Auto Shop two hours prior

Tony was checking the clock. He'd spoken earlier to Father Michaels and had arranged an appointment. The motorcycle ride there was less than ten minutes and he knew that Holt would keep track of every second that he and his sons would waste while he was gone and each would be missing from his weekly check that he was sure was already short of hours.

Tony went to the sink scrubbing the dark grease from his hands doing just well enough to make him passable if he needed to show off to anyone. He didn't think they would judge him harshly for being a working man when times were tough and jobs were scarce.

Tony cleared his throat, Holt looked up to him standing behind the cardboard table. "What do you want, Parker? You aren't done with that brake job already on Mrs. Sanders' car?"

Tony smiled, nodding, "Yep, I finished that two hours ago. I've been working on the Salzman car for the last hour. The spark plugs in that thing are buried. You have to take off the wheel to even-"

"You ain't getting a raise if that is what you are getting to, you might have had great referrals to get this job, but it don't mean you earn anything more because of it. Me and the boys could run this place perfectly happy without you here, you don't forget that!" Holt yelled as he slammed his cards down in frustration at the crap run he'd been having all day.

"Oh no, sir, I'm not asking about a raise. I understand completely that you guys could handle this place."

Holt, who didn't dare tell the boy how full of it he was, knowing his two idiot sons couldn't do an oil job if one held the filter and the other spun to put it on to save their life. "Well, what do you want, don't you know how to take a break, Tony?"

"I don't need breaks, I like thinking and working, it keeps me busy," Tony said smiling.

Holt was motioning with his finger that maybe he best keep talking because he was wasting his time. "Right, I just wanted to say bye, I should be back later today. I have an appointment that I need to get to."

"What does a young kid like you have an appointment for? You getting hitched on your lunch hour or something?"

"No, sir, just the opposite."

"How's that?" Lenny, Holt's oldest son questioned.

"I'm meeting Father Michaels. I've known for a while now that I needed to take the path."

"The path?" Lenny interjected.

"Yeah, Lenny, you know, the one to make you divine."

Lenny laughed, "Grease monkey like you, you really think you are going to be a priest. You got about as good of a chance as I do of becoming one. I can guarantee you I don't have no chance that it will happen. You need to be happy that you got a little green in your pocket and a job to come to in the first place."

Holt stood up walking Tony to the door. "You just get back so you can help work on those last three cars we have on hand. I know the ladies are going to be here after them soon and they aren't going to want to wait any longer than they need to for them."

Tony looked at the three of them and the three cars knowing well that they'd be playing cards and smoking like a chimney late into the night and long past closing time. He wondered how the place had ever stayed open before he came or if some lucky soul who needed a job to support himself and family was here before him. He hoped that they hadn't worked whoever the unlucky guy was to death, he knew that if he got hurt at work it'd be hours before one of these three looked his way to see that there was a problem. He really prayed daily that it would not be the way that his existence continued.

Tony looked to see if anyone cared that he was leaving and not to his surprise...they didn't. He walked out taking a deep breath of the cool air. The fresh air compared to motor oil and gasoline was always refreshing. He didn't complain, there were a million jobs he could do and standing on the rear of a garbage truck did little for his wants of going to work and would not trade what he had for that.

He slid onto his bike strapping his helmet on and cruised down the five blocks to the church. When he pulled in he saw Father Michaels sitting outside starting a smoke. When he saw Tony, he took two quick drags from it and flicked the cherry off sliding it back into his pack.

"Good afternoon, Mr. Parker, how are you doing today?"

"I'm doing good, Father Michaels. Sorry about my clothes, Mr. Holt times my breaks and I didn't have time to get home to change. It takes about as long as getting dressed as it does to get all this grease off my hands."

"Mr. Parker, do we really need to go over this again. You come as dirty as you want to if it means you are coming to the house of God. We don't judge those that work, is it that quick for you to forget between Sundays that God worked with his hands to?"

Tony put the kickstand down on his bike. He backed it in between a set of vans. He hopped off putting his helmet around the handlebar and smiled. He took the steps optimistically, hoping that each one was putting him closer to the path that he was truly chosen for. "Sorry I just worry too much what people think about me sometimes, sorry."

"Get inside, Mr. Parker, I've got a helluva day ahead of me."

"You have demons on the run, Father Michaels?"

He didn't think about it before he answered, saying the truth was what they were supposed to do anyways. Lying wasn't something they went out of their way to do. "Why, have you been speaking to your brother?"

"No kidding, is that why I haven't seen him in a while, is he okay, is everything going alright? Is there anything I can do, anything at all? I'd give anything to help you out, Father Michaels."

"No, sorry I forget once in a while, not everyone should necessarily know everything about what is going on. Given it is easy to forget as normal as you are that you've been through some serious things."

"I know, but I think it has made me stronger."

"It has killed many, Tony."

Tony popped up on his toes a little patting his chest. "I'm still very much here, Father Michaels."

"Yes, yes, you are here Tony, now tell me what can I do for you today. There aren't too many people out there asking for my time unless they have a demon that they need to get rid of. Do you know anyone with any demons that need dealt with?"

"No, no demons today, thank the lord. I'm here about my papers. As you probably know I submitted my application along with a paper to the church. I want to be a…no…I need to be a priest. I know I am helping people dirtying myself in a garage twelve hours a day, but it isn't enough, I feel like I am better suited for a different kind of work helping people. I feel like there's more that I can do, more that I can do for God."

"Yes, James and Billy both have spoken of it. I have every hope for you and if God feels that you are worthy that he will grant you the appointment to become a priest like your brother and James did so many years ago."

"Well, that is the problem, Father Michaels, I received my papers today."

"You didn't get in, I'm very sorry, you can always reapply, Tony, you know, that, right? There's nothing that you have to take as a no. You can-"

"I don't know if I got in, Father Michaels, that is why I am here. I don't know what happened to my papers that were supposed to come to me. They never made it," Tony said and handed him a stack of acceptance papers.

Father Michaels took them hesitantly, not appreciating the lack of paperwork that had the opportunity occasionally to get confused and sent wrong. He looked at the name it didn't take much to realize it'd been sent wrong. He took a deep breath, remembering patience was divine and anger was for fools. Father Michaels took the papers folding and sliding them into his inside breast pocket. "Follow me, let us check with Sister Judith in the office. Maybe she can shed some light on things. You know the nuns, they all stick together. I think they think that it will keep us priests in line, they won't ever learn."

The two walked into the office. Sister Judith looked over her shoulder, seeing Father Michaels and the scrappy looking young man standing behind him, she worried if someone poked him he might burst as wound up as he looked. "Something that I can do for you, Father Michaels?"

"Yeah, there is something you can do for me. You can find out what this man is supposed to do with the rest of his life."

She opened her mouth to say something. Tony, who wasn't as smooth nor as patient as Father Michaels said, "I applied to be a priest, we are here because the wrong paperwork was sent to me. We want to see if I got in. Can you help us?"

She turned to the files, "Name please."

Tony had to take a deep breath, he felt his heart and worried if he didn't put his hand on it that it very well could explode from his chest. A comforting hand set down on his shoulder. "You are going to be fine, I was there and a million other priests have been to. Remember, regardless of the answers you receive, you will be no different. You will still be able to help the church but you might not find it going down the avenues that you thought-"

"Father Michaels you aren't filling me with a lot of confidence, sir."

The nun cleared her throat, still waiting for the name. "Name please?"

"Sorry, Tony...I mean Anthony Parker

She went through until she found the file she had been searching for. She pulled it out, wanting to open it and give the good news, but figured if there was a chance that it wasn't going to be good that she might be best to not make any assumptions. She walked to Father Michaels and handed it to him. He smiled, "Thank you, Sister Judith, we'll go to an office and finish conducting our business. We don't want to take up any more of your time."

"I signed up for a lifetime, Father Michaels. Makes no difference to me if I am helping you or filing papers as long as I am helping someone."

"Have a good day, Sister Judith."

The two walked into an office. Tony felt like he was in trouble for some reason when he sat down and the door clicked shut. Father Michaels patted him on the shoulder and he jumped a foot. He took a seat setting the envelope down on the table. Tony couldn't take his eyes off it. "Tony, would you like to read it or would you like me to?"

Tony reached out for the envelope. His hand was shaking uncontrollably, he tried to play it off but couldn't think of anything clever to say. Tony opened the papers the first three pages were the essay he'd been asked to write about why he should be part of the church and what they thought he could contribute to the church. The first line broke his heart as he read the words we regret to inform you that you have not been selected. Tony looked up, he was trying to be a man about it, but could already feel his lip quivering. "Why didn't I get in? What else do I need to do to be worthy, to get in?"

Father Michaels took the papers looking over the rest of the pages. When he looked up, he didn't feel bad so much as guilty. "I'm sorry, Tony, you can still go back to trying to get selected but I don't feel you are going to have much of a chance."

"Why, what is it?"

"The incident when you were young, it was documented, they all are. The church looks through those records; they know we had to perform an exorcism to save you. To save everyone, they don't blame you by any means, they aren't scared of you, or consider you a threat, but they do not allow you to become a member. I hoped that maybe they would see past it, with your brother being in the church, being a member of it in such a high-ranking position at that."

"So, I can reapply?"

"You can but I don't think they are going to change their minds. This wasn't reviewed by the normal staff. This went all the way up the chain of command. The bishop probably had this in his hands. I'm not scared of you, your family isn't, but any time you have had a hand in hell it makes it difficult to look past it for them. I encourage you to continue, not to give up. There is a chance I can get you to be a deacon if you would be interested in it?"

Tony was in a daze, he'd said that he hadn't put a lot of hope into it to his girlfriend, his mother, and when his brother had asked, but it was a fib and he had worried about it since the day he dropped the envelope in the mailbox. Tony smiled, looking half sick in the face. He took the papers folding and sliding them into the envelope along with his papers. "Could I get back to you about the position and what I need to do so I can be a deacon?"

"I understand this wasn't easy, if God didn't judge us then he wouldn't be doing his job. If he didn't think you should be a priest he never would have put the thought in your head."

Tony got up thinking about all that he had been through. He didn't want to say it, but he did. "I wonder if Satan is still in me when things happen that I don't like, or they don't go my way. How do we ever know that it is out, that we are completely whole?"

"We don't but I think you are a free man; we just need to try to get past this hurdle. I'm going to make a call up the ladder and see if there is anything I can do. I can't make any promises to you, Tony, but I'm going to do everything I can. I think you would be the perfect priest. We need men who have faced issues in life, who have seen the dark side. If you don't know pain outside of what someone tells you in a text book, then how can you understand what a soul is going through?"

"I'm confident that I have felt all of the pain one needs to, Father Michaels, to be able to understand what they are going through."

"I think you do too, Tony, why don't you go try to clear your head, try not to worry too much. I will give you a call just as soon as I know something. Otherwise, I'll try and swing into Holt's if I can't get ahold of you on the phone, deal?"

Tony nodded, opening the door. He turned back pointing to it as he stepped out. "Open or shut?"

"Open please, I still have plenty of work to do."

Tony smiled, standing there for a second. "Is there really something happening, Father? Demons I mean, are they back again? I have to confess one thing."

He motioned with his hand, out with it.

Tony continued, "I hear voices every so often. They don't ask me to do anything and for years there were drugs they would try which did nothing. I think the closet is still a pathway or that they, just like to taunt me."

And you didn't think that was something you might like to let me in on?" Father Michaels pulled out a flask full of holy water. "You pour every drop of this around your bedroom, the frame and across the entrance. You see or hear anything else you let me know, they don't like to lose and when it came to you they lost big. I can only fear how angry they would be about having the opportunity to be freed from hell and then being sent back. I know what it was like for you with your father, no one seemed too upset when he didn't come back. But only in the smallest comparison do you remember that feeling of telling him something didn't go right and you or Billy had to pass on the bad news to him? Now imagine that being the devil. It gives me shivers just thinking about it, let alone speak about it."

"At least if they are there they deserved it in the first place...failure kind of means the rest of us have a chance to prosper. So many people have had to deal with this burden, it doesn't go away overnight. The dreams which I've had to endure were brutal, Father Michaels. To this day one will sneak its way in, it isn't pleasant. I'm sorry I didn't say anything before. I'll be sure to do what you said with the water, can't hurt even if I'm just blowing things out of proportion right?"

"There is no over exaggeration when it comes to something like this."

Tony smiled, holding up the bottle of water and tucked it into his work overalls. He left the door open as instructed and walked down the long hallway to the outside. Waves of emotions hit him like a Mack Truck. Not feeling worthy, not deserving it, not being smart enough, so many things that his stomach turned making him judge if he'd need to go to the bathroom to puke or if he was going to be all right.

He leaned toward the wall for a second trying to get control of himself and that was when the tears came. His body shook with convulsions. He didn't know what to do to make himself feel better. He feared the papers in his pocket were going to have the same answer regardless of how many times he applied to be a priest. He knew that there was nothing wrong with being a deacon and that he could marry and still be one which was one significant advantage over being a priest, but it still would not be a priest and regardless of how happy Alecia made him it was impossible to overlook the fact that being with her solely meant he couldn't be with God in the way that he wanted.

He wiped at his eyes using a handkerchief, not wanting to look like a raccoon if he got grease on his face from work. He laughed a little trying to get his composure as he thought of that. Holt's boys seemed to make a habit out of looking like idiots on a big scale regularly, between the two of them both had issues completing an oil job. He thought of his job and realized he didn't care if he went back today. If Holt wanted to fire him, let him, they'd not be able to replace him at least anytime soon. There were plenty of unemployed in the state, but they typically weren't skilled labor jobs like his because they all found a way to make it by.

He thought of his girlfriend Alecia and realized her arms were going to be the only thing capable of making him feel any better, he just hoped that she'd be home. Alecia would not expect him for at least another four to five hours. He thought that he might slip into his mothers to follow Father Michaels' orders. If anything happened to his mother it would truly break his heart.

He exited the church, nodding to the priests that were congregating at the entrance to the massive cathedral. He ran to the steps missing James by seconds and tore off down the road.

Tony rolled up to his house, it seemed to have more character compared to the rest. He checked the door, but it was locked. He thought of course, it's locked stupid, your mom wasn't born yesterday and isn't going to leave the door opened in a neighborhood like this. Most of the neighbors in the community that were here back in the seventies knew what happened here and they had thought of Tony as a miracle child. The elderly Italian women in the neighborhood would simply call him bambino di miracolo, which he found out later meant miracle child. He had never felt miraculous growing up. The majority of the time he was just thankful he'd survived his father, the demons, and high school. The number of kids who had heard the rumors had little sympathy for a boy who'd been plagued by demons. The ones who did thought it was cool were usually the ones who donned all black clothing, black lipstick and had serious issues. Those were the ones which he wanted nothing to do with.

Tony stopped standing on the stoop realizing he was daydreaming and probably looked a fool standing there. When he put in the key he almost half sensed that it was going to open on its own. But it didn't and he walked in looking around for his mother. "Ma, you home? Ma?"

No answer came, he'd figured she would be at work, but a hug from someone who cared right now would have meant the world to him. Alecia would do just fine and then some, but the feeling of being held by a parent who cared could make you feel like a kid again... in Tony's case it was one of the "non" demon possessed times he'd like to be transported back to his psyche. He took the stairs to his room quickly realizing it'd been hours and had a smoke, the nicotine coursed through his veins as the smoke made its way in and back out. He watched the smoke going into the air, circling around and making its way back down and into the closet beneath. He realized anyone would come off as completely insane for what he was doing next, but he wasn't anyone and this wasn't any normal house...it had a history.

He pulled the water out uncapping it, wanting it to be ready. "Who's there, what do you want?"

A slow sound of fingernails, but much deeper came from the other side of the door. He could visualize strips of wood being slowly shaved off the back of the door and curling, falling to the ground. Tony kicked the door, "I said what the hell do you want?"

"Everything." Was all that it said, "Our ruler wants everything."

The door began to shake and Tony ran a line of water down the frame and across the closet's entrance, almost half of it spilt as he couldn't keep his control. The scratching became a pounding until it subsided and quit completely. He walked backwards, stumbling onto his bed. He tried to raise his hand to his mouth to take a drag, but his hand had never been so shaky before.

The door began to glow red from beneath and smoke filled the room. Tony looked around coughing on the smoke. He tried to breathe, but it was all he could do not to choke to death. He threw the rest of the water on the door crack and screamed with his last breath, "Stay in hell you bastard, you aren't taking me again! I'm going to become a priest and I'll send abominations like you back to hell every chance I can! My God is a just and good one and he will smite you and your devil."

The water leaked out of the container and the smoke turned black making it impossible to see. Both of Tony's eyes watered and he fell to the floor, unsure what to do. He began crawling for the door and when he got a hand on it, it did not budge. Tony was trying to think on his feet but couldn't figure out anything. One of his crosses hit against his chest. He removed it placing it on the handle and pressing the cross onto the knob. He took a deep breath, turning the knob hoping his faith was enough and when he did it clicked open. Tony watched as the smoke dissipated. He sat up against the door to his room. He didn't waste any time and crawled out of the room. When he thought he had even the slightest of his composure and air back, he stumbled sloppily down the stairs. He left a note thumbtacked to the front door. Tony got on his bike, taking a couple quick breaths not wanting to drop his bike. Had Tony waited, he'd have caught his mother rounding the corner as well as the note being blown away.

Chapter 10

Outside Holt's Garage

Billy left the garage in a hurry looking around. He thought for a moment that Morty could be around and maybe he would be annoyed, but not too annoyed not to accept a ride back to the church. The number of things he currently was worried about were increasing. The main thing besides the devil coming was that they wanted his brother and at the moment he was missing and if he was a target he was not safe!

Not that it was an uncommon sound to him but he could hear the sound of pain, but better explained it was more like torture. He thought about running back into the shop and getting the men, but remembered quite quickly that they and the customers waiting were all demons and that was what the pounding coming from the steel door behind him was. Even if they weren't demons, he figured he'd have a better chance of trying to get the police to come to the ghetto and quickly even if he told them he was a member of the local church.

Billy sucked it up and sprinted into the sound of danger. He ran down an alley where there were four homeless men staggering around, one which Billy wanted to pass quickly. The four walked out staggering, but when the first looked up, his eyes, which were red began turning the actual color. The bloodshot in them was no longer the reddest part of his eyes. His friend and fellow bum saw him and yelled, "What is wrong with you Cletus?"

Cletus looked at him, but only because he was speaking. It had nothing to do with the fact that they knew each other, because currently what was possessing him had no clue who he was. He stared back to Billy approaching...approaching much slower now as he was quite sure what he was looking at. The man put an arm on Cletus' shoulder shaking him gently. He brought up a hand never blinking and wrapped it around the bum's wrist.

Cletus pulled the bum in front of him taking his other hand under the man's scrotum in one fluid motion, lifting him in the air and throwing him as if he were a child's rag doll up and into the brick wall head first. He had thrown him so hard that his head split open on impact. He landed on the ground in a heap of crates, blood gushed from his head. The second bum Greg turned to run away, he didn't care what was going on, he knew it didn't have anything to do with him. The man raised a hand and Greg turned around to stare at Billy dead to rights.

Greg said, "There's no reason the blood bag is able to kill all of the priests."

Cletus hushed him, but Greg said, "You know nothing, there will be no future conversations this man will have."

Billy was already on a ten for adrenaline. He reached down to pick up a two by four but already confident it'd do little good. Cletus laughed loud enough for it to echo down to Billy and out the rear of the alley. Billy looked down at it, he'd seen what happens when you hit a demon, it didn't matter what you hit it with.

His supply was running low, but was still far from out, thank God, he thought, as he pulled out a few of the glass water filled balls. Greg and Cletus both knelt just enough to make what they were doing predictable. They leapt and the distance between Billy and them was fading away with each leap.

Billy pulled holy water balls out and with no worry about himself brought them down hard enough to shatter them on the middle and the end of the board, he could feel shards of glass in his fingers and knew if he lived there'd be plenty of time to get medical care. Cletus growled as he approached, Greg was not far behind. The two demons were running on all fours now taking turns leaping off the walls.

They felt invincible and the hatred they had for Billy was not going to be enough to stop them. Billy hung on to the board. A few slim lines of blood made their way down the board. Billy waited to the last minute until Cletus was within five feet. When he was on his final leap, mouth open, with his arms outstretched toward him Billy brought up the wood stepping back a foot and letting Cletus soar directly underneath him. Billy brought down the board so hard that it snapped over the back of his skull.

His forward progression stopped and he slid in the alleyways gravel to what would have been a painful time if the human were in charge. Greg was still moving, seeing his brother in hell did little to settle him down. He connected with Billy's waist tackling him. The two of them flew backwards and Billy took the full impact.

Greg growled, "We will take it this time, we will take everything! Those of you blood bags which don't want to be under our dark lord can be dealt with immediately. It will be a beautiful thing when your world dies as you know it and we can rule it in slavery the way we want to."

Billy tried to push up, but Greg slammed him back down to the ground, using a hammer fist strike to the man's chest. His head slammed into the road, a rock made its way through the skin on the back of his head and in between being repeatedly hit on the ground, knew there was blood and that he had little time left before fighting back would not be an option. Billy frantically reached into his coat pocket. He took three more glass holy water balls and screamed," Go back to hell demon!"

Greg snarled ready to take one final blow and put the priest out of his misery and deliver him to evil. He placed both hands above his head wrapped together and ready to bring them down with a force Billy knew would probably finish him. When he looked as if he was bringing his arms down Billy squeezed with all he had shattering the holy water balls in his hand.

The pain of the glass was welcomed because he would know that his hit would carry the force of a heavyweight boxer. Billy swung, connecting with his jaw. The hit sent him off and he rolled. When he tried to get back up and tackle Billy again, Billy wiped the water on his knee and when the demon tried to connect his hands around Billy's waist, found a knee waiting for him. Billy brought up his leg as hard as he could leaving all the weight on his free foot. He connected perfectly with the man's nose, sending him stumbling backwards, a rainbow of blood flew above him and back as he went up into the air and his nose was spraying through the entire time.

Billy leapt into the air, landing on him while bringing out his bottle of holy water and ripped the cap off with his teeth spitting it into the air.

Greg's demon screamed and that was when he dumped the water down its throat, followed by running his hand underneath it and did the sign of the cross on his head. Greg screamed in agony and Billy knew that there would be no punishment for putting a demon through the pain he was. Smoke rolled out of his mouth and a red bruise in the sign of a cross instantly appeared as he broke through the demon's defense.

Greg still tried to get up again, but Billy had broken through his barrier. Billy continued to hold him down, "I send you to hell, I denounce you on my earth and you can go back to the damned, as one of Satan's soldiers." Billy was no longer going by church prayers that had been practically carved into his psyche. "You do not belong here, and you must leave, you will not take myself, my friends, my loved ones, or any good soul on Earth, your god is weak and mine is just!"

"You do not have the power to stop us all, you will fall, you are a blood bag puppet, you are nothing but a puppet!"

Billy poured what was left of a canister down its throat. It tried to cough back up the water; Billy could only imagine what it felt like. Billy held his hands over the demon's mouth, smoke poured from between his fingers, but he didn't remove it until the demon's color finally faded and the bum's face went back to a natural red color from the abundance of liquor. When his eyes shot open and all he saw was bloodshot eyes, he let his hands off falling backwards. The man rolled over puking the water and all that he had in his stomach upon the alleyway ground. Billy patted him on the back not sure what he could do for him.

When Cletus started getting back up Billy ran over kicking him in the gut. All the air, he had in his lungs came out with a cry. Cletus landed on his back looking up terrified, non-demonic eyes looking at him and his lip quivering. The demon had decided to try another poor soul. Cletus tried to hold up his hands in defense but could not get over the pain that was gushing through his body. Billy almost felt guilty for their pain had it not been for the fact he had just saved both of their lives and God knows how many of the others. Cletus began to cry, "Please don't hurt me, I'll go to church, I'll go to service, father, just please don't hurt me, please, we ain't got anything!"

Billy took one of the man's hands pulling him up to his feet. He repeated the process for Greg and when they were both on their feet, pulled out his wallet handing each of them a ten-dollar bill. "The two of you go get something to eat, don't drink it, or I'll know, you understand me?"

The two both nodded nervously reaching out with shaking hands. When the priest made no moves, and showed no trickery they each snatched it making the money disappear. Neither man waited long after taking the cash before running down the alleyway. Each of them staring at each other trying to figure out what the hell had just happened.

Billy watched as they disappeared around the alley and rested against a brick wall for a few minutes. They'd come outside of homes before, they'd taken the innocent but nothing like this in years, not since his youth.

The screams that he had heard before had not dwindled. The original one sounded like it was now being accompanied by another. He looked behind him to make sure there was no other new threat. When the screams slowed down, he realized he was wasting time he didn't have. The fact that the devil was taunting him so regularly meant something bad.

The idea of them going after Tony again made his stomach turn. Billy ran to the edge of the alley looking for the screaming. A steady stream of smoke made its way up into the air. He saw the van that Morty and his crew had been in earlier. Seeing what happened to them didn't necessarily make him feel guilty, but nonetheless didn't want anything to happen.

The dead were surrounding it, so many memories from his youth were rushing back at him. He ran toward the van to see what he could do, one man that was unrecognizable lay on the ground, a horde of the dead surrounded his picked apart body, another hanging out of the side of the van was practically picked clean. He saw the one demon possessed zombie walking away with a film camera in one hand the size of the ones that they used. He walked to the side to see what was going on with the driver and saw something that stole his breath. The van was stuffed with the dead and the last man's screams echoed to him.

Chapter 11

James made his way into the office. Sister Judith was in her seat still and pointed to the hallway that the two men had gone down and where Father Michaels was still. He gave a thumb up and walked down to find Father Michaels looking at a stack of papers in his hands.

James cleared his throat and Father Michaels looked to him, seeing that he'd not had an easy go around. "What it is, Father Clapper?"

"You've known me more than long enough to know you don't need to be formal with me, Father Michaels."

"Then quit wasting both of our time and spit it out, please, James."

"We took care of it, Billy needs stitches, but he isn't smart enough to stop to get them taken care of."

"So, what is he doing with his bad decision-making skills instead of getting his hand looked at, like it should be?"

"He's running after Tony, we dropped him off at the shop where he works. He is a mechanic now; did you know that? The kid wasn't a few feet tall when I met him now he's tall as me, still a skinny punk but regardless."

Father Michaels tried to be patient, but his day had not been stress-free either. "James, can I assume confidently that if Billy is out running around the city with a hole in his hand that there is a reason for it?"

"The demons said that-"

"You mean demon, not demons, right?" Father Michaels said interrupting.

"Oh no, we most definitely had two, trust me, when we saved the brother, the sister threw the brother out the window."

"Was he alright?"

"I leapt right out after him. We dropped him to his dad and then saved her, and removed the second demon. He's making a play though not like usual...he isn't just being annoying or trying to pick at a few souls, this is big, on a big scale!"

"Yes, James, demons, the devil wants everything, got it, where the hell is Billy at, again?"

"They said that they want Tony, that they are looking for him, that they will take him back again."

"He was here just before you left, saying that he thought he'd heard some things at his house. I gave him holy water to spread around the door. It would be good for the two of you to bless the house when time allows."

"Screw the house, Father Michaels, we need to remove them from the house and keep them somewhere else. This isn't even close to being over. I don't know what the next play is but he's got all kinds of things going on. The demon said something about an outsider, not having the chance to get to have all the fun."

"What fun?"

"The killing of priests, Father Michaels," James whispered.

"I know they don't want us to take them back but we don't usually lose anyone...ever. Far be it for me to call your job safe but we win more than we lose."

"Do we win, Father Michaels? These things are already dead. We aren't killing them. We are banishing them back to hell. I fear when one goes down another comes back, it's a horrific situation, but it is one we don't have any choice over. There's only one-way to cure the world and I fear that neither solution is reasonable or possible for that matter."

"Which reasons are those?"

"One, we have no more sinners in the world. Over time there will be less and less people going to hell. It won't take care of what is down there, but I haven't figured out how to actually keep a demon here, kill it, and not kill the host."

"What was your other thought, James?"

"The same thing I pray a hundred time every day …to close the gates of hell for good, like forever and never let them back in. It is truly the only way I can think of to have it be over, to be done."

Father Michaels smiled, he knew that there was something special about the men he picked to do the deeds most didn't or couldn't accomplish. "You are a special one son. I don't think most people think as big as you do, most priests are content with one demon at a time, you want to send all of them to hell and keep them there forever. You have wonderful ideas, you know that, right?"

"Billy was the one that came up with it, Father Michaels. What do you want us to do? I fear Billy won't want to leave after the threats on his brother."

"I wouldn't make him, if there's still a heavy threat here the last thing I'm going to do is send my top priests away. We must protect the church first and foremost."

"So, what do you want us to do?"

"I want you to stay here for now. When Billy makes his way back, take him and I don't care if he kicks and screams to the hospital; you make sure they stitch him up and that he gets disinfected. We aren't going to lose priests because of stupidity and rushing without thinking, it isn't going to do anyone any good."

Chapter 12

Route 66 Motel Los Angeles, California

Laurie sat outside watching the clock, they had another eight minutes before they needed to go punch in. The car was filled with carpoolers all trying to save a buck on gas. A steady stream of smoke made its way from the four down windows, each of the maids were trying to get the last smoke in that they could. There were fifty-two rooms and with the convention going on there would be no empty rooms after this morning's checkout. Days like this were good for making extra tips. A little care today could lead to an extra fifty cents being left on the pillow or a dollar with the big spenders. Laurie watched the clock roll over and took the last of what she could of her smoke.

"Alright ladies, we need to get in there or Mr. Kirby is going to have a conniption fit. Now remember ladies, if we don't clean those rooms, then we don't get their business next time they are back and everything at sixty-six has got to be the best. We didn't work this hard to become a second-rate hotel," Laurie said in a gruff voice, doing the best which she could to mock the man that they all despised.

Stephanie said, "Come on, we better go, or he will lose it if we are late."

The car doors opened to the wood covered station wagon, windows left down to try and help it air out. Laurie did the sign of the cross and kissing the cross she wore around her neck for good luck today. The four entered through the back as they always did. Kirby was checking the clock making sure no one was late and that no one was early. The last thing he was going to do was let someone earn even a minute of overtime. He said, "Good morning, ladies, how are my favorite maids?"

Stephanie looked around pointing at herself and the others, "Excuse me, Kirby, are you talking to us? I wasn't sure if you hired someone else?"

Mr. Kirby took a long drink of his coffee, "You think you are funny, don't you, Stephanie? Just remember there are a lot of perfectly qualified men and women in the greater California area that would be pleased as can be to take your place. You aren't ready to move on and find a new place of employment, are you?"

Stephanie blushed brushing off his comment with both hands. "Oh, Mr. Kirby, why would I ever want to leave a job like this?"

Laurie leaned in and whispered, "He's fired people for less than disrespecting him. You need to keep it down, if you get fired your husband is going to make sure that you don't forget it either."

"Oh please, Sunny isn't going to do anything to me, I have that man tied around my finger," Stephanie said.

"You really want to take that chance?" Laurie questioned.

She opened her mouth to say something when Mr. Kirby dropped her card in the punch machine clocking her in. He handed it to her with a smug grin. "You want to leave this place you just let me know when. I know how difficult it is to wash and change sheets. But now that you are clocked in, you are on my time and you can get to work."

Laurie punched her own card and ushered Stephanie past him so she couldn't dig herself any deeper.

Mr. Kirby hollered after them, "Laurie, you start on the east wing. Stephanie, you head to-"

"The west wing, Mr. Kirby? Why don't we get to work the same sides?"

"Nobody likes a smart ass, Stephanie. You two get going. You make sure you clock out today for lunch. You do a really good job about forgetting that."

"I think it's the stress of the job, Mr. Kirby."

"Would you please, just go!"

Laurie pulled her by the arm, "I can't give you a ride home if you get canned, go clean your rooms, if you get any tip money let me know, we can go grab some McDonalds."

"McDonalds, oh aren't you a big spender. That sounds good though, I love McRibs."

Jack leaned against the sink in the bathroom. He rinsed his fingers under the warm water, daydreaming about what the future or the end of the world was going to look like. He knew double crossing Satan was the right play, but knew if he did there'd just be someone else who stepped up and took his place. He wanted nothing of a world controlled by him, but as the devil had stated it was best to be invited then sent there without an invitation.

He held the straight blade in his hand delicately and started at the base of his neck going up in little one-inch increments, rinsing the glistening blade under the hot water. Jack contemplated running it across his neck and giving God a heads up on what was happening on earth but was pretty sure he'd heard suicide was a one-way ticket to hell. He looked at his chest in the mirror, knife scars, old bullet wounds, and burns covered him proudly. There were very few that he could not still feel when he ran through the memories.

The lightest knocking came at the door and with the scraping sound by his ear and the sound of the water running he didn't hear it. Laurie opened the door slowly, she knew exactly what she could see from years of experience if people were in the heat of the moment and didn't hear the housekeeping knock. She walked in looking at the sheets barely slept in. She shrugged pulling them off just like any other bed when she saw a figure in the mirror to the bathroom and screamed.

Jack cut his neck with the blade cursing beneath his breath. He took one of the bath towels, placing it beneath the warm water and pressed it up against the small wound. He walked out smiling, only with a few remnants of shaving cream still on his cheek that he would not be shaving anyways.

Laurie covered her eyes apologizing. Jack found a pair of pants sliding them on making sure the zip was easy to hear. "I thought I had the door locked, I apologize for the embarrassment which I've caused you."

Laurie opened index and ring finger looking down to see that he was no longer in his boxers. She smiled nervously, not sure she could feel like a bigger jackass than right now. Jack put up his hand, trying to calm her down.

"Please don't tell my manager, sir, I didn't mean to intrude, I was thinking of a million different things I promise. I'm really good at my job; it isn't easy to get work around here, especially something as simple as this to do for a living."

Jack took the black shirt sliding it on, the white collar that priests wore was hanging from his ensemble and her face instantly went green. Laurie did the sign of the cross, saying short prayers under her breath. "Oh, my...never mind, I feel even worse, Father, oh chr-...never mind I'm just going to shut up."

"Are you catholic, ma'am?" Jack asked.

"Since the day I was born, Father..."

"Father Brown, I'm here for a conference, else we don't usually get to stay anywhere this fancy."

Laurie snorted at that comment. "You must not get to live anywhere very nice then, huh, Father Brown?"

He smiled, understanding that he was in a dump. He had more money than he could burn in a lifetime now, but kept to his trade knowing flashing money was only asking for unwanted attention that he did not think warranted this being successful. "Well, ma'am-"

"Laurie, Father Brown, please call me Laurie. I'm sorry I interrupted you, I don't know what is wrong with me, I feel like I'm flustered."

"It is okay, my child, you are just fine. I would have turned five shades of green and have when I walked in on a nun one day changing with her door unlocked. Here I'd thought that maybe I could surprise her giving her some good news about a benefit she'd asked to do and I saw much more than our God would like me to."

"Oh my, I couldn't imagine...until today of course. Have I said that I am sorry, because I really am sorry, Father Brown?"

"Only twelve times, Laurie. Now do you want to finish the room, and I will finish cleaning up this mess? I've got a small wound to tend to."

"I am so sorry about that."

She backed up tripping on the bed, Laurie put a hand out catching a chair to a small work desk. She collapsed rolling off the side of the bed, the chair atop of her and his suit coat. She laughed snorting not sure that there was a higher level of embarrassment.

Laurie pushed the chair off her and lifted the jacket. Two leather straps were wound around the back of the chair, she looked down to see that they weren't straps so much as cut leather, the type that had been sewn and was currently holding two of the biggest matching silenced pistols that she had ever seen. She looked up confused, "Father Brown, why do you-"

The kind look on the father's face was now melted away. His understanding, humble face was filled with a rage, she was not expecting. She took the pistols with her backing up on her hands and butt doing a crab walk that would make people wonder if she was drunk. She pulled one of the pistols when Jack started his approach. Laurie aimed it center mass getting her balance and on her knees.

Jack said, "You need to flick the safety off, right there on the side."

She turned the gun to the side to see what he was talking about. When she found it, she went to flip it off, but a blinding light hit her in the eyes. She never felt the blade of his razor as it was so quick. The only thing she could feel was what felt like a warm shower running down her neck. She dropped the pistol, the fact that she was dying had not yet registered, nor the fact that the shower was her own blood. Jack took a handful of her hair dipping a pinky in it with his free hand and drew a cross on her head. He knelt still holding her up, Laurie's eyes were beginning to get glassy. Jack whispered close enough for his lips to brush her ear. "Laurie, I hope for your sake that you see God, you aren't going to want to be on Earth for what is next."

She could barely articulate anything but managed to say, "I don't understand, Father. Why?"

Jack took one of the pistols from her and placed it to her temple. "Don't make me the last thing you see. I don't want anyone judging you."

She tried to say something else, but Jack pulled the trigger twice, the twenty-two unloaded behind her ear. Neither one of the bullets exited, and that was why he kept this one on him for close and dirty work. A small trail of smoke came out of the side of her head where the barrel had been.

Jack let go of her and she fell to the floor. He took the rig from the floor, sliding it on; he'd half expected this trip to be boring with all the details he'd already been able to obtain. The day before he had tapped their phone. He knew the two priests were headed to a house to deal with a demon, something a few days ago, he would not have second-guessed as anything but fake. Jack finished dressing, half expecting the woman to become an act of God and have an angel warrior come down and cut his head off for the sins he'd committed.

When she didn't move, he got his suit coat and collar in place. Jack adjusted his guns until he could raise his arms and no one would see the two pistols tucked beneath it. He took the do not disturb sign off the knob and placed it on the outside door.

Chapter 13

Milton's Residence, Los Angeles

Carter pulled to a stop a few blocks away. The two young priests walked side by side to the house. It didn't matter how many times they've been requested to go into a home it always was like the first time. They knocked lightly, waiting for an answer, a voice that sounded as raspy as one could scream through the door, "Get out of here now or you will be an uninvited guest!"

"Mrs. Milton, Mr. Milton, are you there, can you please open the door for us?" Carter asked.

No answer came back, then a scream came that was so loud it could have cut through the house's door. "We need to get in there and we need to do it now!" Nathaniel yelled.

"Yes, then we better get in there, huh?" Carter replied.

Jack had been tailing the two priests for the last few days. He watched the men talking outside of the house. The neighborhood wasn't the type he was foreign to. There had been plenty of rich folks in his time that had hired him happily to off their significant others.

Jack watched them, indiscreetly reading a newspaper, he adjusted his seat and felt the pistol sitting next to his ribs and thought how easy this could have been if the man in charge of his hit list didn't need it to be clean and void of questions. He was used to people investigating his work he'd performed, like the police and FBI, but not God himself.

Another scream came, the two of them didn't hesitate and each put a shoulder into the door. Jack thought that he'd be happy if the demon at this house took out the pair of priests. The door flung open when they put their force into it. They spilled onto the living room floor and a shadow came across passing over them slamming the door hard enough to shake the house. They watched as the door shut, seeing their briefcases and supplies being shut out and most likely locked outside.

Carter got up to a knee crawling over to the knob. He went to grab it when Nathaniel saw it turning bright red in just seconds. He leapt, knocking Carter over and pointing to the knob.

"Would you look at that Nathaniel; it's going to melt soon. I hope you packed heavy because we aren't going to get to do any reloading. Just to make sure they know that the door will not be opening. The deadbolt began to twist and the chain seemed to be held by an invisible set of fingers as it rose and slid into place, taunting them.

A muffled scream came from the kitchen, the two got to their feet, both wishing they'd have not set their gear down outside. There was no such thing as having too much. Each demon was different, some easier than others. Each boy took a calming breath to think things over. They rose to their feet when the scream came again. Each of them pulled a cross from their breast pocket and walked in to see what was happening.

A woman, whom they could only assume was Mrs. Milton was pressed up against the wall. Her metal chair had consumed her, looking more like a medieval restraint device than a chair. The four legs were wrapped around her and pressed into the drywall behind her. The seat was pressed against her stomach tightly and the backrest of the chair was down, making her legs immobile.

"Well, you don't see that every day now do you?" Carter whispered.

"We don't have time to screw around, come on, Carter."

Nathaniel walked across to the chair, pulling a bottle of holy water and sprinkling it on the steel. Smoke began to rise and neither of them had any doubt they were burning the evil and forcing it out of the object. The chair began to buckle when he threw a second handful of water onto it. They took the chair throwing it into the living room. Mrs. Milton now free fell to the ground. She brushed the black hair from her sweat-drenched face. "You have any idea how long I have been here like this. He either forgot about me or just didn't care."

"Is your son still here?" Nathaniel asked.

"I don't have any idea. I saw him go by the kitchen a few times unsure what he was up to and then I haven't seen him since. I don't know what happened, he's such a good boy, I don't know what they want with him. Can you free him, can you get that damnation from hell out of my son and our house?"

"Is it just you here and your son?" Nathaniel asked.

"I don't know if Pat is home or not. I'd say not. We just thought that he had the stomach flu. He'd been in his room for two days, he'd never been so quiet. Finally, I couldn't bear to wait any longer to see what was wrong with him. I went into his room and there he was on the bed, well he wasn't exactly on the bed. He was floating above it. How was he doing that?"

"Your son more than likely is possessed. It is the only way that I've ever seen it done before. I am sorry to tell you that, but I think for sure that's what it is. We will do our best to get him back. Is there another door that you can leave through before he comes back?" Carter asked.

"Yes, I'll try going out the back-sliding door."

They nodded, watching her go to the door. She reached to unlock it when a laughing came from upstairs. It bellowed, filling the house until it was all that could be heard. The deepest voice they'd ever heard screamed at the top of its lungs. "No one leaves, not even the woman!"

She put both hands on the door, pulling on the knob until it finally snapped off. She flew backwards, landing on her rear in between the two priests. They knelt to help her up when a dark shadow came from behind them wrapping its hands around her throat. Mrs. Milton's eyes turned from shocked at falling on the floor to those being killed from suffocation. Carter screamed, "Holy water, now!"

The two reached into their breast pockets biting the corks from the vials filled with the blessed water and spitting them to the side. They turned the vials downwards aiming it directly at her throat, but the water did not so much as spill a drop. They looked at each other confused, never having a demon do this before the woman slid from between them. They each reached for her feet at the last second missing and losing their balance falling onto the floor. They looked up, watching as her heels disappeared around the corner to the kitchen. The two stumbled up to their feet clumsily, dropping the vials, the water finally coming free from it spilling on the floor. "Get up, Carter, we need to go, now!"

The two ran around the corner following her blindly with no regards for the two of themselves. The demon stood at the top of the steps smiling, it's face a mixture of pale white with red veins that almost glowed even in the shadows from the top of the steps. The two looked at each other watching as Mrs. Milton went up the staircase. The demon did little if nothing to keep her from banging her head on each of the steps as she flew up and out of sight. It started laughing a hideous sound if ever they'd heard one.

"What do you want to do?" Carter asked.

"What do you think we do? We send it back to hell! Come on, let's get going. She needs our help."

The two marched for the stairs and the demon lifted his hands pulling the royal oak banister from its place. He brought up his hands and then back down quickly; Carter had mere seconds to leap out of the way before the wood almost impaled him.

He hit hard rolling and pulling out a vile not taking a minute to think about it and hurled a bottle of holy water up to the top of the staircase at him. It dived out of the way, but he hadn't been aiming for it. Carter's throw landed exactly where he wanted and that was three feet above him. The glass shattered on the hardwood that lined the ceiling and walls. It cracked open and rained down upon the demon. It screamed as the holy water covered its skin, giving it an unwanted blessing. It screamed a yell filled with agony and torture, making both priests cover their ears. Carter went to pull a second vial when he watched the ground beneath him become very small and far away.

The demon raised his arms, sending him to the ceiling where he hit with enough force to knock the wind from him. Carter tried to say something, but the demon waved his hands again sending him to the glass chandelier, ruining and breaking it, leaving shards of glass protruding from everywhere. He tried to say something, but the demon took him around in a circle and back into the glass stabbing him in many spots. He tried to hold the wounds, but there were too many for his hands to cover. He looked to Nathaniel, who looked like a lost puppy. He sprinted for the stairs, but the demon waved his free hand, sending him into the wall breaking the drywall all the way down to his feet. He got back control not ready to give up on his friend.

The demon yelled, "Die you puppet, die, die now!"

Nathaniel took his coat off and the demon smiled, playing with him. Carter watched as he was being played like a puppet suspended in midair. The demon yelled, "you'll do no damage with such a foolish thing, what were you thinking stupid boy?"

Nathaniel never lost his grin, trying to hide exactly how fearful he was for his friend's fate. He brought the jacket down on the ground, smashing it into the wood steps, to be sure he was getting what he wanted he smashed the heel of his dress shoe onto each one of the coat's pockets. Carter yelled, "Put me down you abomination!"

The demon looked at him and that was when Nathaniel knelt to take his coat and sprinted up the last three stairs leaping onto the demon. The coat was soaking wet with holy water. Nathaniel hit him hard covering his face with the suit jacket. The two of them crashed hard into the floor, sliding to a stop. When the demon tried to rise Nathaniel brought up one single fist wrapped with a crucifix around his hand and brought it down into the nose of the demon, it groaned when the punch collided sending it back hard where it struck the back of its head.

Carter screamed this time as he fell. Nathaniel looked over his shoulder and saw the outcome happen a thousand times before gravity could finish its job. Carter kicked and screamed in the air as he fell to the ground below. The banister now missing, left a line of railing poles that had been snapped off and left jagged. Carter closed his eyes, trying to cover his face as he came down, he might as well have had wood arrows shot at him because when his plummet ended, so did his screams. Nathaniel tried to say something, but choked on each scream. Carter jerked wildly once before he came to a rest. The wood poles once white were now a crimson red, which protruded out of the back of Carter's neck, spine, gut, and hip. Blood dripped from Carter's mouth and down the poles, Nathaniel watched as a tear made its way down his eye and rolling off his nose dripping into a growing pool of blood.

A laughing came now, the demon could sense his hate and pain and fed on it. He loved every second of this and was growing stronger with it. Nathaniel tied off the coat so that he wouldn't be able to shake it loose from his head. Nathaniel screamed, "You're going back to hell, tell Satan that we said hello!"

"The Devil will see you soon," Nathaniel said. "My Lord, you are all powerful, you are God, you are Father. We beg you through the intercession and help of the archangels Michael, Raphael, and Gabriel, for the deliverance of our brothers and sisters who are enslaved by the evil one. All saints of Heaven, come to our aid. My Lord, you are all powerful, you are God, you are Father. We beg you through the intercession and help of the archangels Michael, Raphael, and Gabriel, for the deliverance of our brothers and sisters who are enslaved by the evil one. All saints of Heaven, come to our aid."

The demon screamed now and this was a scream that was worse than anything he had ever heard at least since his last exorcism. A red light exploded from under the jacket and his mouth, going up above him and then straight back down. The scream subsided and he realized that the horrific scream that had been there was no longer.

This scream was a new one, one that sounded like it was coming from a teenager, one scared, tired, and very confused teen. Nathaniel unwrapped the coat, the boy looked at him with blue eyes, not a red stain in them. His skin went slowly back to normal until he had the normal olive complexion. Nathaniel reached to pat the kid on the head, but he crab walked backwards trying to figure things out in only seconds. The priest whom he'd never seen before was bloodied and sweating profusely. "Robert, Robert, is that you, are you back, baby?" Mrs. Milton asked with tears filling her voice.

"What, what is happening, mom? Who is this guy?"

"Oh, thank you, Jesus, thank you, Fathers-"

She stopped speaking when she saw Carter limp and still in place. Nathaniel turned around slowly walking down the steps. His chest was getting tight with each step to where his partner and friend lie suspended. He ignored the boy, there was nothing else that they needed. He placed a hand on his friends back, kneeling next to him, resting his head on him, unconcerned about the blood dripping from his body. "Dear Lord, Eternal rest grant unto them, O Lord, and let perpetual light shine upon them. May they rest in peace."

Mrs. Milton kissed her son on the head squeezing his shoulder and engulfing him into a hug that she'd been wanting to give him for days. "I am so happy that you are back, I love you, Robert. I love you so much, you were so different I...I...I was so scared, so terrified of you. You stay here, we are going to call the doctor to come for you."

"I feel fine, mom."

"You floated, you did horrible things, you are getting looked at. You stay here for a minute."

She walked down nervously trying to take in visually what she was seeing. The guilt and pain, knowing the men had risked their lives to save her and her son was not something easily dealt with. She placed a hand on his shoulder, "I am so sorry, Father, I never would have called if I thought that anything like this could have possibly happened."

He looked up to her nodding his head. He said matter of factly, "You would have died, he would have killed, the world would have been a darker place for it, ma'am. Or he would have taken you and your husband over."

"Is there someone I can call; is there something I can do?"

"You can call the hospital. He needs to be pronounced, time of death and then he'll go to the morgue and then be delivered to the church where we can put him to rest."

"Father, thank you, I, I didn't, I never would, I mean...I'm so sorry about the priest.

"Thank you for saving me from whatever it was. The last thing I remember was getting home from school. I don't have any idea what happened after that," Robert said.

Nathaniel looked back to the boy. "Go with God, and pray that you stay in the dark. I fear you would not want to share any memories with the demon in your head."

Nathaniel squeezed Carter's shoulder one last time wishing it was himself and not his best friend. When he reached for the door, he was able to open it this time. He thought of how many times the two of them had been locked inside of demon possessed homes together and wished this was just like any other day.

He walked outside to the home's front step, sitting down, he'd been trying to quit, but felt this warranted a cheat smoke. He pulled one from the pack looking around in a daze and not paying attention to the bystanders that had gathered around the house. He let out a long drag tapping the ashes in the yard, the sound of the sirens coming brought him out of his daze. When the ambulance and officers arrived, he let them in the house, staying for a statement. The police were skeptical until they saw the railing to the stairs and the bloody prints on the ceilings where they were twenty feet high. After he saw that Carter was properly taken care of and given the care that he respected, he headed back to their car, this time carrying both of their briefcases hand in hand, head and shoulders sunken.

Chapter 14

Route 66 Motel Los Angeles, California

Mr. Kirby had the phone on his shoulder running his finger down the list of rooms. He'd heard from eight this morning and it was only eleven. Most guests preferred to get an early breakfast because no one ever wanted to skip a free meal, especially when they didn't have to exit their pajamas to do it. Stephanie walked by, smiling when she saw Jack walking through the lobby. He nodded and Mr. Kirby whistled to her to wait for him. Jack set down his briefcase on the counter, pulling out a fifty-dollar bill to take care of the night. Mr. Kirby looked at it rubbing his hands on it. "Church must be doing pretty good nowadays, Father Smith, is it?"

Jack nodded, Smith was his favorite name, and there were a billion of them. Jack smiled, "The church is always the best place to be my son. God knows all and sees all, therefore He is divine."

Mr. Kirby, who had not been to church in twenty years suddenly got wet and clammy hands. He smiled nervously for he had absolutely no clue what in the hell to say to something like that. He nodded slowly and Jack pushed it further taking his hands in his. "Do you believe in our great and holy leader, the man who shows us our way? You know it is never too late to take the path of the church, are you married?"

Kirby shook his head no. "I'm not catholic, Father Smith. I haven't been to church in so long that I don't even remember what denomination I am, bless my mother's heart, I couldn't think of it if my life relied on it."

Stephanie was standing in the corner biting her lip and trying not to laugh aloud. Kirby looked to her shooting daggers. "You come to church if you ever feel like enlightening your life my son."

Jack thought he deserved an Oscar for his performance. Hired by Satan to go around and kill the priests on this list. He couldn't be further from what he was pretending to be. It would not take very much to start off laughing at this point.

Kirby pushed the receipt toward him with his free hand praying the stranger would remove his hands from his. "I'll keep service in mind later today, who knows, maybe I will get off in time to make it happen."

Stephanie choked on her laugh, "You know Mr. Kirby, I'm sure that I could give you a ride in our carpool. You know that Laurie is quite kind about it, maybe the three of us could all go to church together, sing songs, hold hands, thank God for all that he is."

Jack clapped his hands together, taking the receipt and making it disappear. "Now that is something, isn't it, I love to see faith at work."

He looked up at the cameras feeling a quick wave of nausea. Jack wasn't stupid and wouldn't be surprised if this came back and bit him in the ass. He had two issues here to deal with and then would be on his way to somewhere new and leave this all behind.

Stephanie brought him back out of it, "What church are you out of, Father?"

He tried to come up with a name and smiled. "I come from St. Mary's Church, Las Vegas, Nevada diocese. I'll hopefully be heading back there very soon."

Jack took his belongings and headed out the door. Kirby stared at her, Stephanie was confident that she had never seen his face so red before. "Mr. Kirby, are you okay?"

He gripped the sides of the counter and veins which she had not seen on the man began to pop out of his forearms and head. "Go find Laurie before I strangle you in the towel closet, I can't stand you! You would burn at the cross if you tried to walk into the church. You mock me in front of a priest and try to belittle me...do you have any idea how embarrassing that is?"

"Probably no more than what I deal with on a daily basis from you. You stay back here behind your little counter and think of what you will get for lying to a priest."

"You just make sure that you tell your buddy Laurie that I want to talk to her the minute you find her. I don't know what the hell she's been doing all morning, but it is ridiculous. I won't stand for it whatsoever. She should have done way more rooms by now!"

Stephanie wanted to say something, but could already see the look that first Laurie would give her and then her husband would give her if she got fired again for her mouth. She spun around, hurrying down to Laurie's side of the building. She walked slowly down the three halls looking for her, but didn't see her cart. She checked all the rooms on the floor that didn't have a do not disturb sign on them. She went down, finding which ones that were not occupied the evening before and started going through the ones on her cart that had already been checked off. She was beginning to worry something fierce about her best friend. She looked at the sheet seeing the room the priest had been in and opened the door slowly.

Chapter 15

Tony opened his eyes, but it was dark. He tried to wait patiently for things to come into focus, but they didn't like the darkness that was like the black of night and there was no light to be seen. When he tried reaching for the lamp he found his arms would not work. Tony could feel something tight around his wrists, but wasn't sure what it was. He started feeling nervous when a licking sensation began on each of his fingers, not one tongue running across each fingertip, but many tongues and what he could only assume were multiple mouths.

"Who's there? Alecia, are you there? Babe, what are you doing?"

Tony leaned his head up trying to still make shapes out of nothing. A small set of lights finally made their appearance. Tony had to squint as they seemed like they were miles away, something that his brain couldn't comprehend at the moment. As the two lights got closer he realized they most likely weren't lights but instead were a set of eyes, a red pair of eyes and even in the dark, he could tell these were eyes filled with anger, the type that had been there for longer than he had been on Earth. "What do you want, what do you want, leave me alone! Get out of here, leave, leave me alone!"

"We can't leave you alone, we need something from you."

Tony tried to speak, but the licking sensation on his fingers had turned into light nibbling, and the nibbling very soon became biting. As the light began to come back to him Tony realized he was on a large stone slab, the walls were red. He looked down at his hands and saw creatures like he could only describe as a lizard-like object, but covered with symbols that he'd never seen before. The monsters began ripping his fingers off one at a time. Tony screamed buckling under the pain, but his restraints gave him nothing to move and the pain was intense enough to keep him from passing out. He could feel warm pools beneath both hands of his blood as they chewed.

"Oh God, would you stop, please, stop!"

The figure with the red eyes put a finger to his lips, it was warm at first, but very quickly began to burn his lips when he rested his finger or whatever the appendage was. It almost scolded him when it spoke. "Do not say his name, he is not here, nor will he ever come to hell."

Tony tried to scream again, but choked on his scream when a red glowing knife came out of nowhere. He realized as smoke danced up into the air that it was not red, at least that probably was not its normal color. It was frozen in its current state by the degree of heat that it was smoldering at. "What do you want! What is it, you can't have anything of mine!"

It dug the blade deep into his gut. Tony could only explain it as his innards boiling from the inside. Just when he thought that it could not be worse the being started running the blade up to his heart. Tony tried to say something, but watched in awe as the being which he was now sure was a demon disappeared quickly before his eyes, taking refuge in his stomach. Tony could feel cold sweat which he didn't think would be possible in hell. The light hairs singed on his stomach running from his navel to his neck. He watched the wound close before his very eyes, he could feel bile in the back of his throat. "Get out of me, leave me, you damned creation!"

A voice that came from his own mouth said, "We will go nowhere, you are ours, again."

"You were removed, they sent you back to hell!"

"They tried, didn't they. You are ours I am going to eat your soul while I wait for my master."

Tony screamed at the top of his lungs. The lights came back and he jumped a foot swinging and falling out of the small bed. He hit hard on the wood floor, squeezing his eyes shut, unable to see anything. The light seemed like it was the brightest thing he had ever seen. He couldn't make sense of the soft voice, he was still trapped in hell. When he finally focused his eyes, he saw a figure looking like it was hovering over him, something gold catching a reflection and bouncing the bright light even further into his eyes.

Tony got up from the floor, his long black hair hit the back of his neck and it was soaking wet. Every feeling and sound was driving him insane it felt like nails were being pounded into his ear and claws were pulling at his flesh. He gasped for breath before the words finally made sense.

"Tony, Tony, honey, are you alright? What's wrong with you, what happened, what was it, Tony?"

Tony squinted, looking up seeing the reflecting object was a gold cross, one that he'd seen almost every day for the last two years. "Alecia is that you, is that you?"

He ran his hands across his stomach feeling no incision, no pain, nothing bad at all. Two hands soft and delicate took his cheeks. She hushed him dropping to her knees when she felt it was safe. "It was just a bad dream, it was just a bad dream, I'm sorry I woke you abruptly from that, but I was sure that you were going to have a heart attack if you kept going at the rate you were going, honey."

"I...I don't know what to say. It wasn't a bad dream, it was...it was more, it was hell, I was in hell. I felt everything, every gouge, they tore my fingers off and a demon cut me and took home in my stomach."

"That's absolutely horrible. I knew that they were working you too hard at the shop, you need to tell them that a guy can only fix so many cars in a day."

Tony rolled to his side debating if he was going to puke for a second. He pushed up and climbed back onto the now dampened bed. "Sorry about your sheets, sometimes when hell finds me, I sweat."

"Forget about the sheets, good lord in heaven, that is the last thing that I am worried about. I'm worried about you!"

"I'm okay, they aren't as bad as they used to be."

"That makes me feel a lot better that this is considered good. Have you seen a doctor about this, I mean they might be able to-"

"I've been dealing with this since I was five years old, Alecia, I assure you, I have tried everything. Doctors, shrinks, I've tried sleeping pills, and being stuck, unable to wake is not the way to take on these dreams. Thank you for caring though and bringing me back from that. I don't want you to freak out every time I stay over, maybe we shouldn't-"

"Anthony Parker if you finish that sentence, I'll be forced to tell your mother of all the sins we've committed unmarried on top of it. What do you think she would do to you?"

He smiled, holding up his hand, looking at it, the shakes had subsided and he reached down to his jeans pulling out a pack of smokes. He took one out collapsing back on the bed and lighting it. "She'd make the devil look like a lightweight if you told her that."

"Do you want me to take you to a doctor?"

"Yeah with what insurance, we could go to the free clinic and then I'll make someone confused when I explain my entire history to them. No, there's nothing that can be done. I'm sorry, but I got baggage to deal with, Alecia. I just don't know how to help it or what to do about it. It's better than when I was younger, and I like to think that by the time that I have kids that maybe, just maybe I'll be normal," Tony said.

"I don't know if you'll ever truly be normal, sweetheart. Who are you planning on having all these babies with sweetie? I don't know that I'm ready to start popping them out of the oven just yet. We need money, and a house, and-"

"Whoa, Alecia, slow down would you, I wasn't thinking today, we could practice when I'm feeling a little bit better though as much as you want. You know we could really make sure that we've got it down for when the time counts."

"You realize that we'll need your work boots soon to walk around in here if you talk very much more crap. You really are shut down because of that dream. You sure you don't want to talk about it?"

"I don't want you to have to deal with what I'm dealing with, trust me."

"If we are going to be together forever, then it is something that I need to deal with."

"What if I told you that there was a time when I was younger where Satan or one of his was inside me. I did some horrible things. I was only stopped because of my brother, his best friend, priests, my own mom and neighbor. It was a big effort."

"Satan was inside of you? I don't understand is that why you have all those tattoos everywhere on you?"

"They thought that the reason I got possessed, the reason that they took me over was because of my age and maybe the lack of a cross on me. My brother, his buddy, and everyone else but my dad all had one. As soon as I was old enough I started getting them."

"You've never spoken about your dad before."

"Drunk, abusive, mean, likes to hit, likes to punch, likes to throw, gamble. When the devil snuck into my house the only good thing it seemed to do was push him out. When my mother came out from the hospital that he put her in, we never saw him again. She didn't ask around, we didn't try and find him and he never came back. We thought that the devil might have taken him where he belonged. No one really missed him, about the only people that ever came to ask about him were those that he owed money to. He loved to gamble. I'm sure he'd like to say he was always happy when he was up, but he was never up, all he ever did was lose, and he'd lose everything too not just something small, he went all the way."

"I guess it is a good thing, then that he's gone from your life?"

"Blessing in disguise. What time do you work tonight, you aren't going to be late because I slept over are you?"

"I don't work till seven, I get out at midnight. You know I heard if you walk a damsel in distress to work through the hood that you can get a free piece of cherry pie a la mode. Would you know anyone interested in that?"

"I'd love it, you give me a minute to shower, I already stink from sitting in a hot garage all day, the last thing I want to do is go there when I smell like this. Do me a favor while I jump in really quick, would you?"

"You want me to get you some of your spare clothes?"

"No, but see if you can find one of those damsels in distress for me. I love pie and ice cream," Tony laughed as he ducked into the shower slamming the door, keeping a work boot from nailing him in his rear.

"You better be good to me Alecia. You never know when the call is going to come from the church."

"Okay, Father Tony you just get washed off and hurry up so I'm not late to work."

"I got my bike, we'll be fine."

"A gentleman walks a lady."

He poked his head out of the door with a smile. "But isn't it so much more fun riding on my bike?"

"Hurry up trouble maker!"

Tony showered feeling a million times better. Soon the two of them were strolling hand on hand through the streets of Chicago. He'd begged her to ride the bike but she did not want her hair messed up from the helmet. Tony and she held hands as they walked, neither of them looked like they had a dollar between the two of them to steal and they were not bothered by any of the vagrants roaming the streets. Tony opened the door to the restaurant smiling, finally letting go of her hand. She leaned in whispering, "What kind of pie did you want, were you set on the cherry and ice cream, Tony?"

"You just get me a slice of whatever they aren't going to miss. The last thing I want you to do is to get in trouble over giving me something sweet."

"They can't afford to fire me, Tony, I don't steal, I come in on time, and I don't do drugs in the backroom. They need to make me a manager at some point."

Tony took her hand pulling her back, making her squeal and gave her a smooch on the cheek. Her cheeks grew red as they always did when he embarrassed her and she headed to the back, the sound of a time clock being punched a second later echoed loudly. Tony dropped into a seat looking around at the patrons of the establishment. Tired was all that he saw, men and women who'd worked more than a person should be asked to sat in the seats. They shoveled the food into their mouths, some not taking a break from smoking to enjoy their meal. Cold beer for those who were done for the day and steaming coffee for those not lucky enough to be done for the day or who were headed to start their night shift. Even though he was as poor as the next person he knew that being appreciative at such a young age of having things like love and God in his life were as valuable as all the money in existence.

He thought back to her joke about the church not needing Father Tony and felt a tinge of pain. He opened his jean jacket, pulling out three sheets of paper. He unfolded them seeing words scribbled and scratched across the top of it for essay ideas. He smiled as he read it for the millionth time. He loved his girlfriend as much as life itself, but he had loved the church longer, not just because of what they had done for him, but for what it did for all the families across the world. He thought of James and Billy and knew that his brother would be turning wrenches just like himself if he had not been accepted by the church. Billy had been more book smart and with his time as an altar boy and assisting Father Michaels in every manner available had been basically groomed since ten years old or before for the church.

He set the papers aside when Alecia came back with the pie. She set it and a large bowl of ice cream down kissing him on the head and said, "I might be able to get you a to-go burger if you are here at midnight when I get off. You feel free to bring the bike though I don't want to walk these streets that time of night, like at all."

"No worries, I'll swing by and check on my mom before she goes to bed and then I'll be over to get you. Don't you go keeping me up all night, though, I have to be at the shop at six in the morning or I'll never hear the end of it. I think they assume because I can show up on time and I don't drink that it's okay to have me open it up every morning."

"It isn't because everyone else is too hungover?"

"It is what it is, they were nice enough to train me how to do it, most kids would have to pay for an apprenticeship to be able to do that. It probably doesn't hurt that I had a stack of references all from my favorite neighborhood priests."

"Lucky you, try to be good. See you tonight."

Tony nodded and she rustled his hair, which he hated because it was long and still wet and made him look somewhat insane when it was not properly combed. She laughed as he tried to blow the wet strands from his face, all he could do was shake his head. He cut into his reward pulling a bite away from his pie and dug into the ice cream trying his best to keep them balanced on the fork at the same time.

"Hey, hey asshole, there's maggots in that pie," a man he'd never seen nor spoken to before said.

Tony looked at him, an elderly man smiling at him. The man smiled, his teeth were gone, nothing but gums left that looked diseased. "Excuse me, did you say something?"

"Yeah you, moron, that pie, you're eating maggots, they're everywhere, the ice cream too."

Tony shook his head, ignoring the man. He looked down at his spoon seeing exactly that though. He dropped it making it clatter on the table, spilling the bite everywhere. Two men looked at him curiously. Tony tried to ignore them, pulling napkins to wipe up the pie, he moved it around ensuring that he was not seeing maggots and that his eyes were playing tricks on him. "Real funny old man, why don't you mind your own business."

Tony turned around ignoring the man, but unsure if he could try and eat the ice cream. The old man leaned forward, elbows on the table, he removed his sunglasses his eyes were glowing red. "That wouldn't be any fun would it, Tony?"

Tony snapped his head around seeing the eyes and didn't say anything, he didn't want to ask questions that might be answered. The two men that had been watching him earlier whispered, "Hey, kid, you alright?"

Tony gave a thumb up trying not to look over his shoulder back at the elderly man who had begun laughing now. Tony looked around, but no one seemed to hear the man, his laughter grew until it was all that he could hear. He turned around in his seat when he could take no more and yelled, "Would you shut up, damn it!"

The man's eyes were back to a soft green and he jumped visibly shaken in his seat choking on his tea. He pointed to himself and Tony shook his head hating that he couldn't trust his eyes. "Sorry, I...I think that maybe I'm hearing things."

He looked to the pickup window for the waitresses and saw Alecia motioning with her hands for him to keep it down. He smiled uneasily giving a less than confident, okay sign. One of the two men next to him shifted toward Tony. "You doin all right over there pal? You ain't gonna cause any trouble, are you?"

"Just want to eat my pie and keep to myself if that is all right with you."

"Sure, as rain, but you need to quit yelling at folks or you're going to start making people nervous, you aren't on any of those drugs are you, making you all crazy in the head, now are you?"

Tony held up two fingers mocking a boy scout. "Sane as can be expected, sir."

The other man shook uncontrollably. He smiled to Tony now, his brown eyes turned black and then red in a matter of seconds. He brought up a giant bite of pie chewing with his mouth open, maggots that only Tony and the stranger could see were falling out of his mouth. The man's voice grew raspy and said, "We're going to murder your girlfriend in the alley, cut her guts out in the alley, the cute one, right? This is some good pie."

Tony looked at Alecia thinking the two of them could run, they could outrun the two goliaths if they left right now. The other man looked to his friend Eric, "What the hell are you saying? I'm not doing anyth-"

Eric set down his fork wiping at his face and took his butter knife flipping it around and with his free hand caught his friend Rick off guard. He brought down the knife with all the force he had into his friend's hand. His friend screamed, but no one in the diner seemed to notice. Tony saw a police officer enjoying a burger and fries. He was still chewing and didn't seem to be bothered by the man screaming. Tony tried to get up, but the man said, "Sit down, or your mother is supper. I bet she'd be delicious."

Tony got up flinging his chair back. Eric, the man with demon's eyes, got up meeting him toe to toe. Blood was covering the table and the man had tears in his eyes screaming at the top of his lungs. Eric looked at him sideways like, he was unable to understand why he was being so rude and so loud. He took a finger running it across the lips of the man with a knife through his hand. Tony watched as the man's lips melted away into nothing. He clawed at his lips, his eyes were filling with tears and it was apparent he was losing his mind, something Tony felt the two of them were able to share. "Who, who are you?" Tony asked.

The man stepped forward, sniffing and smiling. "You aren't pure, are you? You've been taken before, I can smell it, we've got a hold of your soul...you just don't know it yet do you? We'll be taking it back very soon I think."

"You're insane," Tony pulled off his jacket, rolling his sleeves and exposing the crosses he'd had tattooed on his forearms with the words, May God Keep Me Safe Beneath Each of Them. "You will not catch me without a cross ever again, demon, now go back to hell where you belong."

"We'll see each other again very soon, I promise you!" Eric's eyes faded back to their normal brown color.

Tony took a step back looking around the diner. Every single person was staring at him, half with a fork hanging out of their mouths or mid-chew on their meal. Tony looked in front of him realizing that it hadn't happened. Alecia was looking at him in shock whispering WTF to him, her face had never looked so rosy before and he didn't know if at the moment it was from anger or embarrassment. He opened his mouth to say something, but everyone in the shop had sucked the words from his mouth. He looked down at the two men who he thought he'd been talking to and seeing being tortured and the two of them looked as normal as could be. The police officer was standing up looking annoyed for being troubled to stop eating his meal. Tony looked around, unsure what to do. He ran out of the diner not saying anything else.

Tears started to make their way down his face. He wasn't sure if they were demons or if he was finally going crazy from all the medications and previous possession. He sprinted through the street, he tried not to look at the bums on the street, but when he did he saw their faces distorted and shriveled even worse than usual. One screamed to him, "We're gonna cut Joan's throat tonight, and then we're going to eat her soul!"

The group laughed as he sprinted away. A patrol car pulled up in front of his sprint and came to a stop. The officer from the diner had radioed in to have someone on the lookout for a man that appeared to be absolutely deranged. Tony tried to turn to run but the officer who had been in the diner was there holding a gun in one hand and a baton in the other. Tony held up his hands, "I didn't do nothing, I didn't do anything, I'm just trying to go home, I swear, I just wanna go home!"

The officer from the diner shook his head not letting him know he'd probably be detained this evening. He stood shoulder to shoulder, looking left then right. The officer's eyes turned black and a shadow came over his face. "We're going to take a ride to hell where you belong, Tony, get in the car."

Tony was unable to control what he thought was real or not, took a swing connecting with the officer's jaw and sending him to the ground. The patrolman from the car hesitated zero seconds, bringing down his baton into the back of Tony's skull sending everything black. Everything he heard from then on sounded like it was coming to him through a tunnel. "Hey, you alright, Travis? He knocked the hell out of you."

"I'm fine, I've been hit harder, look at him, he's in a cold sweat, that kids on drugs, probably crack."

Tony felt two arms, taking his biceps and could just barely see his feet as he was dragged to the car and thrown in but not until a pair of handcuffs were placed on him making it feel like his wrists were going to explode from the pressure.

Chapter 16

LAPD

"Los Angeles Police Department, how can I direct your call?"

"There's a dead body in my hotel, it is one of my staff."

"Is the killer still on the premises?"

"I don't know who the hell the killer is, I don't know what happened, two hours ago, she clocked in and now she is dead. Her friend found her and almost lost her mind. She's in the backroom shaking at this point and mumbling something. I'm pretty sure she's going to quit."

"Please hold, I'll get someone on the line for you to speak to, we need to make sure we got everything answered."

Mr. Kirby tried to reply, but the hold music came on and Lionel Richie was singing Hello to him. The front desk officer punched in for homicide. Detective Dursky was sitting around a desk listening to two other detectives tell him a tale that he didn't believe for anything. Dursky smiled uninterested in their line of bull. When the phone rang, he said a silent prayer that he didn't have to sit here any longer and that if there wasn't a reason to leave, he still was going to go check in on something, on anything, hell he figured he could help someone in robbery if that was the case.

Dursky held up a finger, smiling and took the phone. The other two detectives walked off still recounting the story or at least how they remembered it. "Detective Dursky, how may I help you?"

"It's Larry, detective, I think I got a fresh one for you, you got the time?"

"Wouldn't have answered if I was on a case, Larry, you know any details?"

"Nope, just that it is a hotel, a friend found her, the manager is freaking out and they don't have a clue if the killer is still on the grounds."

"Send two cars over there, no lights, no commotion, they can tape off the room and make sure that there's no one there to ruin my scene. Maybe there'll be someone who screws up and comes back, maybe we will get lucky."

"You really think somebody would be that stupid?"

"I never start off assuming someone is dumb, but the things I've seen criminals do is mind baffling sometimes."

"I think everyone is, I mean everyone! You should hear the things I have to do; it is enough to make you lose your mind. You deal with them once they have a tag on their toe, you just have to speak to the dead and figure out who killed them."

"Yeah, there's nothing crazy I ever need to deal with. I'll head down to the scene, you let the manager know we are on it, stay out of the room, the entire staff doesn't need to go in there to say they saw the dead girl."

"You don't want to talk to him, at all?"

"Not particularly, if something comes up or the officers on the scene see something or hear something they can reach me. I got car five-sixty-two today just have dispatch channel you over."

"Yeah, I can do that, good luck out there."

Route 66 Motel Los Angeles, California

Dursky pulled up to the gravel parking lot in back. He never went in the front if he could avoid it, at least if he was going to a business. People were themselves and pleasant, even when something bad had happened. He liked throwing them off their guard; customer oriented employees had been trained to be polite and respectful to customers. If he came in from the back, they knew there would be no cause for them to think they hadn't already been there and meaning that they'd already collected their money.

Detective Dursky got out looking around to see no one. He dropped his butt in the gravel grinding it out with his worn wingtip dress shoe. Stephanie looked up, seeing the cheap two-piece suit, the cropped short blonde haircut, and then eyes that were way too active. People looking around that much were either police or criminals. The fact that he had state plates and a Crown Victoria painted deep navy blue couldn't scream louder that he was the police, the fact that she and Laurie had lived in the ghetto when they were just starting out on their own did not make it anything but easier to see him. They'd had more drug busts in their neighborhood, car part scandals, chop shops...not the kind you took your car to so it could be fixed, but where stolen cars were dismantled and what parts were good on it were liquidated to area mechanics who were even less honest than the people stealing them.

Dursky saw Stephanie and from the looks of her and the pile of butts by her feet, knew that she'd been placed outside. He already knew the answer to his question, but he had to work people into answering questions and typically making them start out here with a few yes answers got them into the habit of it. Dursky asked, "Excuse me ma'am, do you work here?"

"Yes, I do, or I did, I don't know, I think that I'm gonna quit."

"You need me to call someone for you?"

"What are they going to do, you got a priest you can talk to for me? Maybe they can do something to make me feel better, about the only thing that would make me feel any better is to know that Laurie was in heaven looking down on me and was in no pain...anymore," she pulled out a fresh smoke dropping the one she was still smoking off on the pile.

"My name is Detective Joey Dursky. You can call me Detective or

Detective Dursky.”

“Joey?”

“It’s what my parents put on my birth certificate, hand to God.”

“Bet that made dating hard sometimes?”

“I'm happily married I’ll have you know, three kids too,” Dursky said with the hint of a smile, trying to ease some of the tension she was feeling.

“Really, I'm sorry, I say stupid things when I'm upset.”

“No worries, I'm just kidding, I'm as single as they come. But I'm always thinking I’ll find someone right if I'm patient enough. Who doesn’t want to fall in love with someone who does this kind of a thing for a career. I do my best not to take my work home with me, but I don’t give up until I find the son of a-”

“You are going to find out who did this to Laurie aren’t you? I mean, you’ll figure out who it was and why they did it? People don’t murder someone for no reason, right?”

Dursky shrugged, “I can’t say, we can’t ask the dead what happened, all I try to do is to put the pieces together and figure out what happened to them. I know it isn’t easy and it won’t be easy tomorrow either. You strike me, as someone working that knows what she is doing. Can you help me with any information before I go talk to your boss?”

“Sure, it was one of her rooms. Mr. Kirby, or Peter, or Dick as I like to call him stuck us on different wings of the hotel. If we aren’t working like the world will end, then he has a conniption fit. I don’t know what his problem is. He can quite literally sit on his fat ass all day flirting with the ladies coming in and out but doesn’t do a damn thing. If we try to catch just one extra smoke break, he’ll kill us.”

Dursky perked up at that and Stephanie wasn’t stupid. She shooed the idea out of his head before he could even make an assumption about him. "It was the priest, Detective Dursky, at least I'd put my money on it."

"A priest is who you think killed her?"

"You go in there and tell me you don't think a man of God did it, or at least someone trying to impersonate a man of God?"

"Would you be able to show me to the room? You don't have to go in, I promise. You can come straight back out here. I'd rather not have anyone in there. Is there something religious going on in the room?"

Stephanie didn't say anything as she took one last drag that would have killed him and flicked it uncaring where it went. They walked through the hallway and as they got closer realized it was getting quieter with each passing step. "You guys get rid of the people in these rooms, Stephanie?"

"Mr. Kirby did, he moved everyone to the opposite wing. He knew that if anyone saw the yellow tape that the next stop they'd be going to would be the front office to check out and leave. People don't want to stay in a horror story, they want a place that makes them happy about not being in their own bed."

"Does he like this job, Mr. Kirby that is?"

"Just check out the room and you won't have to be questioning him in the manner that you are planning on. I don't mean to tell you your place or job, but it is what it is. He's a jerk but he does his job and wouldn't lay a hand on any of us. He knows better, our husbands would beat him to a pulp if we came home bruised."

He saw the yellow tape from down the hall and put a hand on her shoulder. "There's no reason for you to go in if you don't want to. I know you aren't going to get any joy from it and would be disgusted if you did. Are you going to be okay getting back? Do you want me to send one of the uniforms with you, Stephanie?"

"I can walk back, I'm in no hurry to go back outside and sit. I really appreciate that you care, that you aren't just writing her off as another dead maid that got killed by some crazy guy and you just assume that he left state."

"I either catch them or they come up dead, there is no in-between. I haven't been on the job long enough to not care. I don't plan on doing it if I give up on catching the perps. If I do, I sure as hell am not going to go and be a quitter when it comes to catching people that have killed others."

Stephanie didn't ask, she just walked forward, gripping the man around the shoulders and squeezed him until her arms wouldn't give her any more power with which to do so. She let go pulling him down by his tie a foot kissed his forehead and whispered, "Catch that son of a bitch please. I don't want to have to tell her husband that they are going to get away with it."

"They aren't going to, don't worry, okay. I mean worry, and beware of your surroundings, but-"

She cut him off smiling weakly. "It is okay, Detective Dursky. Just do your best, I have faith in you."

Dursky watched her walking down the hallway slowly, feeling guilt and pain even though there was no way for him to have foreseen this or not doing anything to prevent it. He felt a small hope and calmness and watched as Stephanie walked into a light...the only light that was finding its way into the hallway. Her white maids uniform almost made her glow until she had been engulfed into it.

A cough came from behind him and brought him back to the world that needed dealing with. "I'm aware it needs looked at. Just let me have a moment of faith, would you?"

The younger of the two officers couldn't help himself. "So, what's the upside to doing this job? I mean, if it is tearing you apart, what do you get out of it?"

"I didn't take this job to be happy; I took it to help people, and if that means I have some issues to work through then that is what I do. There isn't a lot of options somedays, but to just put your head down and push through it."

He looked at the younger cop and saw that his face wasn't much off from looking like a lime Jell-O. The veteran officer who knew better than to talk with detectives or to ask questions said, "You mind if we step outside, I don't think the rookie here can make it much longer. He's already lost everything he ate this morning and probably last night as well. Gonna need to toughen up if he ever wants to try and be the cop that his dad and brothers are."

"In my defense, I've never seen anything like that, sir, and you looked like you were about a second away from blowing your breakfast all over the place as well."

"I had gas, you needed a tampon."

"You guys head out, I don't need anyone babysitting me. I've done this enough that I'm not worried about losing anything. Head out before I waste any more of my day. Kid if you got a weak stomach you stick to robbery and crimes when you decide you want to wear a suit every day."

He gave a thumb up keeping a steady hand on the side of his stomach, trying not to draw attention to it. When they left, he brought out a pair of gloves, blowing in them and getting them shook out. He pulled them tight and began doing his ritual of making sure each finger was in place. He pulled out his cassette player and headphones placing them on. Dursky got a tape out sliding in a Bach violin concerto. He hit play and began to float away into the room.

Dursky took slow, steady breaths, the room was not yet rank in any way and she hadn't been here long enough to make a difference. He wasn't sure how long he was going to be there so he turned the air conditioner on after checking out the room, not yet letting himself look at the scene. When he spun around, he took in the room, the kill, the blood, and everything in-between at once as a whole. He would run through a list of kills in his head upon first look trying to find anything that matched up to a previous murder he had worked in the past.

He had not dealt with many serial killers and he was fine with that. The one time which he had, it had not been a difficult case; the man had been so blood hungry that he could not control his own urges. He had gone through an apartment complex in the ghetto and while Dursky was investigating one building and the killer was five over making a second horror scene. When he had stepped out for a smoke it had not taken a very long time to find him. The man had come out with a duffel bag filled to the brim with skulls that he had cut the eyeballs from. Dursky had always wondered if it was for religious reasons or from insanity. He never had the chance to find out. One of the police on scene screamed for him to stop and he choked himself with the barrel of a three fifty-seven revolver squeezing one off in the commons area. No one tried very hard to get him to stop, he only had to fire once to blow the back of his head off and cover the pavement with his brain and bits of skull. When he'd pulled the gun, he had let go of the bag he'd been carrying. A dozen or more heads rolled from it. He had been confident that if he hadn't done the job himself that one of the officers would have helped him with it, or made sure he didn't move on from the cell that he would be placed in.

Joey shook the memories from his head, there was no decapitation here, no this was something different and it seemed like it had a meaning to it. He lifted the sheets seeing there were no stains on them. He walked the ground looking around seeing no stains that weren't from blood and was confident after looking for a few minutes that at least she had not been sexually molested. Dursky checked her eyes, each had a coin in them. He lifted her eyelids with his pen just to make sure that indeed she did have her eyeballs in place. He lifted her chin, looking at her head, seeing the cross drawn upside down on it. He knew that probably wasn't a good thing and that to date there'd never really been a demon-loving cult who was devout enough to do anything in the devil's name. He took a few steps back, pulling out a Polaroid camera and snapping off a few shots before the real photographers got here and messed up the scene.

Dursky looked at her trying to figure out why he'd done what he had. She had nothing on but a white sheet that had been placed neatly to cover her privates. A nail through each of her hands and feet were keeping her in place replicating Jesus' crucifixion to the letter. He waved the picture until it came to be and slid it in his pocket. Dursky looked through the entire room, dusting for prints seeing nothing at all. He went into the bathroom to see if any type of evidence might have been left in there but saw nothing. Dursky took a few breaths, trying to get his head around what was happening.

He punched the wall already frustrated knowing the priest gimmick wouldn't pan out. People pretended to be someone else every day of their lives out in Los Angeles. No one was doing what they wanted to for a living, they were strictly working toward the career that they wanted to truly do. The waitress or barista that wanted to be an actor, the cook who was a screenplay writer, the surf pro shop guy who was just waiting to become a pro surfer. It didn't matter where you went if the person wasn't wearing stripes or carrying a badge they most likely weren't doing what they wanted to. He didn't want anything else for himself but to catch the bad guy and when he went to sleep be able to close his eyes and not see all the death and destruction that was waiting for him every so often.

He let out a deep breath on the mirror, seeing the outline. Dursky started to breath hot air as fast as he could in the corner. The first thing he saw were upside down crosses. When he continued, he started to see letters on the mirror. The first row was on the bottom was "me", he went up higher seeing "stop" and he had to stand on the toilet to make his breath get that far where the word "must" was coming up in the fogged over glass. He got off the toilet seat thinking about it and wasn't sure it would be much help. "Must stop me" but what the hell did that mean he thought. There were no clues to what he'd be doing next, where he was going, or why he killed a maid in a crappy hotel.

He walked back out front to the lobby, Mr. Kirby was resting on his stool looking like he was going to be sick. "Detective Dursky is it?"

Dursky nodded, walking over, shaking hands and handed him a business card. "Do you know what time that room, checked out?"

Kirby opened his mouth, but Dursky saw the logbook on the counter and spun it around. He ran his finger down until he saw the Father Smith written neatly, as was the signature, probably because it wasn't practiced often enough to be used to it and to write it sloppily like any other average American did. Dursky checked his watch, seeing it'd only been a few hours and unless he was flying would more than likely still be in the city now. Dursky looked around the lobby and two black cameras stood out as plain as day to be seen. Dursky pointed to the cameras. "You going to make my job easier and tell me those cameras work?"

Mr. Kirby nodded his head, "Damn right they do, those are the smallest VHS recording cameras money can buy, they are barely a foot long. You can't get no better when it comes to security, we care about our customers...and our employees, don't forget about that, we need them, we need all of them nice and safe. You want to see the footage, Detective Dursky?"

"No, I was just making sure that they worked for your sake, Mr. Kirby."

Mr. Kirby looked at them and then back at Dursky slowly. He couldn't help himself and asked slowly and cautiously. "You just kidding about that, aren't you, detective?"

Dursky took a steadying breath, trying to remain calm. He gritted his teeth, unsure if he could refrain from reaching around and saving the world from this waste of space by strangling him with his bare hands. "Yes, Mr. Kirby, that would be just fantastic if you can set me up somewhere with a place to watch it."

"I can't leave you alone in the back room with the safe, it is against company policy."

"I'm just looking for the guy's face, I don't care, come on."

Mr. Kirby slid in the tape hitting rewind and smiled, pointing back to it, "Don't even need to press play once it is done it starts on its own. A real miracle of modern day ingenuity, detective."

Dursky, more of a reader was unimpressed and shrugged, waiting for the tape to play. He leaned forward on his knees slapping the television's side. "Piece of crap, what's wrong with the screen?"

"This is a top of the line Zenith television I'll have you know. It doesn't get any better than that,"

"What the hell is wrong with the screen, what is going on?"

Mr. Kirby leaned in pausing the tape multiple times and the two of them squinted together, "Well what in the Sam hill is wrong with this damn thing? I check this every morning, twice if the drawer is short any money. You can't find good help, especially them that don't speeko no Ingles if you know what I mean?'

Dursky did know, but after five years in the army, right out of high school, he had little concern for the color of the people around him. He knew damn well a coward could come in any color including white, and so could a hero. Dursky got close when he turned it around seeing the fine dress of the man. "You have any churches around here by chance? I wonder if he was on his way to a church, or if that is just his disguise to blend in, or to be ignored. I can't imagine how many people don't want to speak to a priest out of fear that they think he will give him a tongue lashing for not going to church on a regular basis. I know I've missed more than one service lately."

"There's a church about five miles from here. It is one of the larger ones in the city."

Chapter 17

St. Mary's Cathedral, Los Angeles

Nathaniel pulled around to the back of the church. He let go of the steering wheel. His hands were white from squeezing it tight enough to cut off circulation. He hadn't even realized he'd been doing so until now. The blood began to pour back into his hands and felt like someone was stabbing him with needles. He had cried the entire way back. He knew how close they were, they'd had to rely on one another for years knowing if they wanted to see the next day's sun they had to stick together and take care of each other. The best thing he could compare it to was someone cutting off his arm. The idea that he would be forced to either be paired up with a new priest...one which he did not know...one that he could not trust right away made him feel even worse. He had been going through each step of their day since they entered the room. They had done everything right, but he knew as well that there was never a guaranteed path he should take each time going in. The demons he felt were close, that when they came to Earth they came here with all the knowledge of the demons before them. They always seemed like they knew something new each time.

Father Edwards was waiting patiently in the parking lot on a bench tapping out what was left of his tobacco from a pipe before making it disappear into a carrying case. He used his cane for the walk to the car. Nathaniel had not seen him sitting there, and he was a hard man to miss. When he saw the head of the church heading over he realized he needed to get up there. If he walked too far he was going to make himself have a heart attack.

Nathaniel got out of the car holding up a hand for him to stop. "Wait there, Father Edwards, you are just going to need to walk that much further back."

Father Edwards nodded, thankful the young priest was so considerate toward others. "I know what happened, I got a call from the detectives on duty. They wanted to confirm that the two of you had been sent on a church case. Once in a while we get a skeptical officer who is not a big believer. I am fine with people being skeptical, I think it strickens them of some of their power."

"Really?"

"Nah, it's a pain in my butt every time we lose someone and have to go through all this. How are you? I know how close the two of you were. You've been at it for almost your entire careers."

"I'm not sure, I won't lie, I feel like someone cut open my chest and ripped out my heart. I don't know if I'm strong enough to do this job by myself?"

"You've never had to. Either the church will assign a new priest to you or they will leave you on your own."

"But what if I can't do it, Father Edwards? I've never had to fight these things on my own, and they are more evil than ever now."

"I don't disagree about that, the stories the two of you have been relaying have been horrid and I do not have any jealously for your mission in life."

"What about me being on my own, though?"

"It is simple, if God feels that you are capable of doing it on your own then you will. He knows and sees all, he had plans for Carter if he took him. He has a plan, one for all of us."

Nathaniel wiped at his eyes with his shirt sleeve. "Just when I thought I didn't have any other tears to shed."

"Never be embarrassed of them son, we all have our days. Yours is just particularly difficult today, and each day going forward you are going to have new challenges, new issues, but you will always have the church standing behind you with a hand on your shoulder."

Nathaniel, not usually one for showing emotion wrapped his arms around Father Edwards. A new wave of feelings washed over him. "I...I don't know what to do, there's so many of them out there."

Father Edwards knew there wasn't a good answer. There were a lot of them and they would never stop, they'd never quit trying to take Earth until they had taken it and heaven. He patted him on the back hushing him. "You still have about an hour until mass starts. I think you might sit in; it might make you feel better. What have you to say my boy?"

He tried to let go of Father Edwards, but he held onto him for a few more seconds. Father Nathaniel nodded his head. "Yeah...I'll be there, thank you for everything, I really appreciate it."

"It is us that appreciate you, and the work you and Father Carter did. You do things that go above and beyond the call of priests. There's a select few and the weight upon those chosen's shoulders is large...if there's ever any need to talk just say something, please at any time. We will help you through this and push forward. Heavenly Father, allow your son Jesus to come now with the Holy Spirit, the Blessed Virgin Mary, the holy angels and the saints protect us from all harm and to keep all evil spirits from taking revenge on us in any way."

"Father, I thought we were going to go to mass for prayers."

"Not that the others can't use an extra prayer, but you can use all the help you can get. You go get cleaned up, wash the blood from your hands, and join us in the chapel."

Father Nathaniel patted him on the shoulder and headed inside, disappearing into his room.

Father Edwards was making his rounds through the church, he had other priests to do such things, but as he had been told many years ago, if you don't check on things yourself, you can't complain when they aren't done as you wanted. He checked that the coffee and cookies for after the service were ready and out. Sister Harriet had a fresh cup and a chocolate chip...Father Edwards' favorite kind setting out, knowing she'd see him. He used his cane to take the pressure off his old knees, which made the snack that much more difficult to eat. He waved at the young volunteers who were standing ready to help...which he knew were most likely volunteered by their mothers, thinking it would be good for them. They had the day's mass on their handouts for the attendees.

The altar boys were walking toward the back of the church. Father Edwards looked at his watch shaking his head in disappointment. He hollered to the two boys. "You boys don't waste any time getting ready, all right? We don't have time for you to be late. You make sure that you bring up the supplies for communion. Don't take any drinks of the wine either, I'll know."

The two boys looked at each other both knowing he was full of it, but the fear of God watching them sin was enough for the two of them to nod politely. They walked into the rear of the chapel to the changing rooms. The cart was already set up with the wine that would be distributed and the bread chips had been put in the basket. A man was putting the trash away from set up. When he turned around the two boys did not recognize him. The older of the two said, "Hello, Father, are you new here?"

Jack smiled proudly, "No, I've been here for a very long time. I have been away travelling to different churches for the last few years. How long have the two of you been here as altar boys?"

"We've been here a few years, but I've been coming to the church for all our lives. I'm sorry and please...please don't take it wrong, but I can't remember you for anything. You say you've been travelling but you used to be here?"

Jack never lost his beat when talking. "Well, I had a beard back then, and all the time I've spent in the north has left me wearing hats more often so my hair stopped bleaching from the sun and made it go dark. I just thank the lord that I've still got hair to worry about. I just thought that I'd come back and surprise the other priests and help you two boys out with communion by getting it ready. It has been too long since I have been home."

The boy nodded and the younger of the two leaned over and said,

"Ben, I don't think this guy is supposed to be here."

He said it louder than he meant to and Jack had given them his undivided attention. The two watched as he walked forward. He was smiling, but it wasn't one either of them liked. He reached between the two of them locking the door and pulling out the old skeleton key that was in it.

Father Edwards was feeling the day. He walked down the hallway that seemed to get longer each year. He could remember practically running up and down the halls trying to take care of as many things as he could in his youth. He didn't want to give the altar boys too hard of a time because it seemed like only yesterday that he was one of them taking a short drink of the holy wine and worrying that God was going to strike him down, and then tell his parents who would surely put him in a less than desirable position.

He listened outside of Father Nathaniel's room for a few seconds. He could not hear any sobbing. He knocked gently opening the door, unsurprised that it was not locked. The priests typically did not bother one another when in their rooms and were usually in there to pray privately or sleep, else they weren't in there at all. "Father Nathaniel, are you decent?"

Nathaniel was sitting in front of a small, slim mirror adjusting his collar. "I was just finishing getting my suit on. I definitely feel better after a shower and some clean clothes. I said a few prayers for Carter. I hope they take good care of him in heaven...he went too soon and-"

Father Edwards knew he was only going to make himself feel pain again. "Why don't we get going, Father Nathaniel. I can't very well tell the altar boys they need to be early to get ready for church and then not be on time myself, can I?"

"Probably not with a straight face, Father Edwards. I'm all set, can I walk down there with you?"

He nodded and the two made their way down. A priest came around the corner colliding into the two of them. He mumbled his apologies never stopping, but making sure that Father Edwards had not fallen down. Nathaniel was so busy making sure that Father Edwards was okay that by the time he looked to the man who had so rudely ran into them saw that he was gone. "You all right, Father?"

"Yes, thank you, just knocked the wind out of me…unfortunately that doesn't take near the effort that it used to," he said smiling uneasily while patting a very plump belly.

The two went in through the chambers and Father Nathaniel saw the cart sitting by itself. "You want me to get this taken out, Father Edwards? Seems like your altar boys might have forgotten about it this week."

"Those boys, they'll be the death of me. I mean really, they come here a few times a week every week, how hard is it to remember what they are supposed to do? Really, they get the wine filled, then put the bread chips in the basket and then they make sure that we have extras of everything that we might need more of. How difficult is that, really?"

"Hard to say, Father Edwards, you remember what it was like being a young boy, a million things going through your head at every waking minute. You trying to figure out life and how not to get in trouble were your main concerns. It is difficult to keep them focused, I feel. I wouldn't give them too hard of a time, not all of them are planning on taking their vows to God when they graduate."

"Well, I bet if they knew what you got to do the boys would be fighting to be priests."

Nathaniel didn't want to remind him that they'd lost one today, and those looking at what he did with admiration would quickly fade if they knew what they had to do. The things people thought were amazing would only last until they walked a mile in his shoes. Keeping respect for a man who he cherished, he said, "Don't worry, Father Edwards. At least if there isn't an influx of people attempting to be men of the cloth we can skip wasting time on those not truly cut out for the job. The ones who think they got the calling, but truly didn't. Not that I am the one to say if someone is or is not worthy to wear the cloth."

Father Edwards went to open the door which led directly out to the front, but when he twisted the door handle found that it was locked. "Who would lock this door, this door is not to be locked under any circumstances," Father Edwards said, slowly letting his voice rise.

"I have no idea; do you have the extra key for it. I'm sure someone just removed it and didn't even think about it," Father Nathaniel replied.

"Probably, but I don't carry my keys around regularly. You want to see if someone has a set around the bend real quick?"

Nathaniel nodded disappearing and a few minutes later opened the door from the outside. Father Edwards was already pushing the cart out as the door was opened. He saw they had a full house today; the word must have somehow spread that one of the priests residing in the church had been lost. The people of the church didn't get reports of what they did, of course, but rumors spread and they knew that these men helped keep hell at bay and away from them.

The congregation rose to their feet as the two priests made their way out, it filled both men's hearts with goodness seeing it. The support of the followers did more than he could have possibly imagined it would have done. Father Nathaniel looked over to see a hand on his shoulder, but when he looked to see who it was saw nothing. He placed a hand on it unsure what was going on but it was gone. He made a sign of the cross, unsure who was there, but he had a suspicion...or more of a hope that it was Father Carter, who was there with him now, hopefully watching over him and keeping him and the others safe from harm's way.

Father Edwards whispered in his ear, "You look fifty shades of white, are you all right. If you aren't up for service, if you need to rest, then you go ahead and go, you do what you need to do, please. Whatever it is you do it, we want you to be whole again."

"No, I think I'm all right. I can do it, I just...I just felt like there was an old friend there for a moment."

"Just because he's passed doesn't mean that he is gone. We spend such a short time on this earth doing God's will that it doesn't mean we are finished when we pass," Father Edwards said. "Why don't you go ahead and start our service today, if you are up for it I mean, it might do your body good."

Father Nathaniel, who usually wasn't the one to speak at mass walked forward flicking on the microphone to address the crowd. He looked around at the faces, sorrowful expressions were looking at his every feature. He tried to smile, but he didn't have one that he could fake to try and make them feel better. He wasn't ignorant and he knew that if you couldn't be your true self with your congregation you would not be able to do it elsewhere.

He leaned in too far making the microphone scream like nails on a chalkboard. "I'm sorry, I wasn't expecting to speak. A few hours ago, I would not have been able to. I wanted to speak to you about faith, and loss today. I hope that I do you justice, I know exactly how long Father Edwards and the other priests spend on their sermons each week. I will try my best to not let you down. I see your faces; I understand that rumors have already begun to flow freely through the congregation. You want to know details, you want to know what happened, who to blame, what you can do to help, so many questions, so little time. The short and bittersweet is that we lost Father Carter; he died doing his duty to the church. If you want someone to place your blame on, I can only say Satan."

The crowd gasped at this, many started doing the sign of the cross and holding their hands together. Most of them had their rosaries tucked in between their clasped hands. "Keep it down please, yes we all know there is a devil, for if there wasn't one what fear would you have? You might ask what is bittersweet about losing a priest, losing one that you all know worked hand in hand with myself? I can only say that he died doing what he was put on this earth to do. I feel that even though he is gone, he will never be forgotten and while I am in no hurry to join him in heaven, I have every confidence that when our Lord and Creator comes for me, that will be exactly where I find him. This time is dangerous, there is something afoot, but if we stay strong, and faithful the dark wishes of others will fail. You must do your best to have the faith that I know you are capable of. Please bow your heads for we need to pray for those lost, those still fighting and those we will lose who are trying to do well on your behalves."

Father Nathaniel led the prayer going slow not looking up. He'd hooked them from the beginning of the service, and every watchful obeying eye was upon him. He did not want to scare the congregation, but letting people roam around freely unaware of the dangers was not something which he was okay with letting take place.

Chapter 18

Route 66 Motel Los Angeles, California

Dursky was punching in the number to call the precinct up and get back on their way to the church. The officers from earlier came up, the older one first. "Detective, you don't need to send anyone additional to the church, sir."

"What in the hell are you talking about? The man that they had in that room that did the devil's work was dressed like a priest. He's five to ten minutes away from it and has a two-hour head start on us. You give me one good damn reason why we don't send everyone we got there?"

"Because we already have everyone we can spare on their way there?"

Dursky rolled with his fingers for him to keep going, "Get to it, the short version."

St. Mary's Cathedral, Los Angeles

Dursky pulled up slowly, looking out the window to the church. He could only shake his head, even from a block away he could see he wasn't going to be prepared for this. He took out his badge sliding it around his neck on a chain. He tried to take it in, there were twenty medics in the chapel, each of them with a clipboard. A detective he knew went walking past and he gripped his arm. "Mark, what in the hell is going on here? What is going on with the medics?"

"Time of death, Dursky, you know that. They have to declare it so they can make note of when they passed away."

Dursky didn't say anything, he left Mark standing there waiting for another question to come. He walked into the chapel and the fact that he'd never seen this many dead people in one room made his stomach drop to his knees. "Oh my God, what happened?" He whispered.

"You ever hear of the crazies that drank the Kool-Aid, killed every single one of them?"

"Yeah, there's no way a Catholic Church would do that though. You aren't saying that is what happened, right?"

"No, all I can assume is that someone put something deadly inside of the wine glasses, or inside the wine itself. I've never seen anything like this," Mark said.

Dursky gripped at his gut not sure if he was going to be able to keep what was on the inside where it belonged. "Were there any survivors, Mark?"

Mark smiled lightly, "There were a handful of babies, all the children who haven't had their communion before, and some recovering alcoholics that only took the bread survived. By the time the members started passing out in their seats they ran to the phones. At first, they thought it was just a few people that had gotten ill from something, maybe the flu, I don't know what was going through their mind. In my defense, I can't imagine having to look up from a prayer to see people dropping like flies, that'd be torturous to my head. By the time the medics got here everyone who'd touched it was gone. They said that they've never seen a drug or poison act so fast to kill before."

"First thoughts, is there anyone here that you think they might have been after, do you think it was a church reason for trying to do it. Were any of the members in here important enough to send a hitter into the house of God?" Dursky asked.

Mark shrugged, "We've been here less than twenty minutes. I don't have a clue if anyone here is important or not. We are trying to get information on them but other than an envelope for the church gatherings in the offering plate we don't know much about any of them. My guess though is someone is either trying to accomplish a mission or-"

An officer near the dressing room yelled to the two detectives from across the church. "You two better come see this, and do it quick please!"

Dursky thought about it and the fact that there were almost two hundred dead bodies here, and in a few of the saddest cases there were new orphans and widows that made it even worse. Dursky knew if God didn't put a hand on the widow's backs, they would definitely have their lips around a bottle of whatever they could get their hands on tonight. Dursky looked to Mark and shrugged, "You want a part of this, or am I going to do this on my own?"

"That officer has been on the job for two decades. If he says we need to see it, then let's make sure that we aren't screwing anything up. Whoever this guy is I'm either putting him away or putting two in his chest. He can pick how that goes down when we pick him up."

The two headed for the back-dressing room. They looked around not seeing anything. Dursky said, "We'll have more paperwork than the guy that originally had to write the Bible. I thought that you said there was something in here which we needed to see? Where is it, for God sakes?"

The officer pointed to the curtain and neither of them wanted to be the poor bastard to pull it back. When they approached it, they nodded unconfidently to each other and each took a side of the curtain. They pulled them back quickly like a band aid. The breath they were holding when they did it began to burn like a deep fire until each of them realized they weren't breathing but simply holding it in. The two of them seemed to have had the exact same revelation. That something evil was here or had been.

Dursky looked at the boy on the left first, his eyes had not been closed. He pulled down the collar of his dress shirt, he'd never seen hand marks on someone's neck this deep. There was a rage this man was trying to get out, or something else angering him past his breaking point, he thought. Mark was looking at the other boy, "This one wasn't strangled, I don't know what the cause of death was."

Dursky wanted to say check his arms, but this was a ten or twelve-year-old boy not one of the junkies overdosing on skid row. He looked at the way the boy was leaning and slowly pulled back his collar not seeing anything. "Right, just like I said, Dursky, he didn't get strangled."

Dursky pulled his cassock down looking closer at his neck. He ran his gloved hands over the boy's neck seeing nothing but then running his fingertips across the back of the boy's neck he could feel a large lump under the cassock on the rear of his neck. He let go patting the boy on the shoulder not thinking it was a pointless gesture at this point. He looked down at his hand, seeing a Los Angeles International Airport slip of paper in his hand. The number said flight five-sixty-two. "What the hell is that, Dursky?"

"I have no idea, but I think…no, I know that there is something bigger going on. Call the airport, tell the security force there to look at the tape. It is going to look like there is a glitch, like there will be a man they can't focus on. You find out where that is, where he is going. I'm going to try and catch up, you figure it out, you radio me in the car and the airport if I'm not in there. You understand me, Mark, you do it and you do it now!"

"How are you going to get on the plane?"

"I'm going to show them my ID and my gun and they are going to give me a seat to wherever we go and hope that God and the officer's in the next town have a sense of duty. I know I won't have jurisdiction, or a way to bring them back here. But with God as my witness I want to get this guy, I don't know what he's trying to do, a maid, a congregation, priests for God sakes, and doing it all in the house of the Lord, what is he thinking? He's practically paving a one-way path to hell. But he said stop me at the hotel."

"I thought you had to find him on video, that you didn't know where the hell he went?"

"I was going over the room. I honestly found it on accident, he wrote it or something wrote it on the mirror."

"Something?" Mark asked.

"I don't know, it just seems like there is something bigger going on here, something crazy that seems more evil than anything I've worked on before, Mark."

"That is absolutely horrifying to hear considering the kind of things you get called in on."

"I just hope that I can find him, the worse thing about this job is you don't get a call till the body has already hit the floor. I gotta figure out where he's going and what he's doing."

"I'll get on the horn and try to get you a step ahead of him."

Dursky headed out of the dressing room with his head spinning. He was confident the boys walked in on whomever was doing the poisoning to the holy wine. The priests were lying on the floor each of them lying where they'd fallen except for one. Dursky noticed Father Nathaniel lying on his back. His arms were crossed on his chest, two gold coins from the devil were on his eyelids and he had in blood written on his forehead stop him. Dursky whispered to no one that was in earshot, "I'll stop the son of a bitch, Father, I promise you this!"

He leaned down seeing a white business card sticking out of the breast pocket. He went to grip it but realized he'd already removed his gloves. He patted at his pocket for a fresh pair, but was out. Dursky found a pen sliding the cap off and using it like a pair of tweezers and stuck it to the card. In simple Times font it said, In case of emergency, please contact Father Michaels, head of those who do the holy work and send those unworthy of Earth back to hell where they belong, Chicago, Illinois. He turned the card over seeing a simple black cross and the address and phone number to a church in Chicago, Illinois.

He held up the card looking around and ran to the back of the church where he found an office and a telephone he could use. He punched in the numbers knowing it'd be a very awkward conversation but had no choice. If this man could be of any help, he would not look the gift horse in the mouth. He punched in the numbers to reach Father Michaels. He sat there practically bouncing in his chair. "Hello?"

Dursky cleared his throat, "Hello, I'm trying to reach a Father Michaels, please."

"Try no harder because I am him. Is there something I can do for you?"

"I have something I am supposed to tell you I think."

"I can imagine that, because this number is private, and I know everyone alive who has it. I fear you got this number from one of them, are they in the hospital? Were they hurt, were they at your home trying to-"

"I fear I have bad news to break to you Father Michaels. My name is Detective Dursky, I'm from the Los Angeles Police Department. I was responding to a case which led me to the church here. If you haven't already seen it, you will, or it will be in the papers tomorrow and on the news tonight. We have the scene locked down currently."

"The scene, the news, the papers, can you give me some information, my heart's going to explode if you don't give a few details. There are many people in the church and I care for them all but there were a handful of men at that church who are very special."

"We were at a hotel this morning, a man dressed like a priest took a maid and crucified her and left her there. In his hotel room, it said to stop him, I'm unsure if he's speaking of himself or-"

"The Devil, dare I say?"

"Look, I just wanted to call and let you know that this seems personal. None of the victims seemed to receive any special attention except for one young priest with a full head of hair, and looks like he'd blow over in the wind."

"Check his breast pocket for his wallet please. I fear I already know who it is though."

"Can you hold for a few minutes while I run back?"

"Please hurry, I need to know."

Dursky jogged back up sliding in between a slew of people. He ran back to Father Nathaniel's coat, pulling his identification from his wallet and made his way back to the phone. "It says Nathaniel Hufford, twenty-nine-years old, does that sound like someone that you know?" Dursky asked. He held the phone wanting to ask more questions but refused to take a moment from the man if he needed it. There was no doubt that there was sobbing coming from the other end. Dursky waited just as long as he could before finally asking, "Can I assume that he is someone that you know of, Father Michaels?"

"He was one of the ones that you don't want to lose. We have so few of these men that there aren't any we can afford to be without. He's going to be missed and I don't know how his partner is going to be able to live without him."

"Can you give me a description, or a name, because he wasn't the only priest, Father Michaels."

"What details aren't you giving me, Detective, please don't hold anything back, you aren't helping make me feel any better. Are you saying that there was more than one?"

Dursky looked at the sign on the desk saying thank you for not smoking and flipped it upside down. He put a smoke to his lips, lighting it and leaned back. "It was all the priests, it was almost the entire congregation, there was a poisoning at the service today."

A thud, which Dursky assumed, was Father Michaels dropping the receiver upon hearing the news. He waited for him to pick it up when a second much heavier thud came. Screaming came from the background that he could hear, followed by a man screaming to call an ambulance. James picked up the phone. "Who is this, what did you say to him."

"This is Detective Dursky I'm just doing what this business card said to do. I was on my way to the airport, but if I was able to help someone in any way at all, or give some type of warning to anyone to be careful of this psycho then that was what I was going to do."

"What are you talking about, what does the card say?" James asked, looking down at Father Michaels lying on the ground, but feeling better when he could see his chest rising up and down, his eyes were beginning to flutter and realized that he was all right, that he had just fainted.

"You make sure you are sitting down. I don't need anyone else to pass out on me. It says, In case of emergency, please contact Father Michaels, head of those who do the holy work and send those unworthy of Earth back to hell where they belong. Maybe you can do me the justice of telling me what the hell this card is talking about, send what back to hell? Who was this Father Nathaniel?"

"He was one of the few in the states that regularly sends demons back to hell. When they come to Earth and take over one of the innocents, we cast them back to hell where they belong."

"So, you're talking about real life demons?"

"Those are the only kind of demons that I know about, Detective Dursky. I thank you for calling him, but what made him go down?"

"He asked if only Nathaniel was the one I found. I had broken the news to him that it was all the priests and the congregation. We think…no we are sure that the only thing that could have happened was poison in the wine. Only those who skipped drinking the wine because of age or previous demons haunting them were excused from it. Everyone else here died. There had to have been over two hundred people. It is the worst thing that I have ever seen. Women, children, men, teenagers, everyone. Whoever did it had absolutely no concern for their victims."

"He was one of the only two who were in charge of fighting demons in the California area. Things have been picking up here lately. My partner got hurt and had issues of his own to temporarily deal with and I haven't seen him since. If I need to go warn him of danger, you say the word."

"I don't know, the man had a ticket on him I assume, and one of the boys must have ripped the stub off when he was being killed in the dressing room."

"One of the altar boys? Good lord, what is wrong with this man? Who kills innocent boys?"

"I'd say confidently that there is a lot wrong with him. I can call back when I have more information, can I give you my name. The precinct can get a hold of me at any time, day or night, regardless of where I am."

"I thought you were getting on a plane?"

"I will in just the minute I find out where he is going," Dursky said as calmly as he could. He was having a hell of a time wrapping his head around all the information which he was hearing for the first time.

Mark poked his head in the door, and the words coming off his lips felt like a blow to the head. "He's heading to Chicago, Dursky. I had the security team run the number and then they checked the flight video. Guess what they saw when they watched the tape, or guess what they didn't see when they saw the tape. The bastard has to be doing something to the videos I just don't know what?"

"I don't know either, but he's doing something, and it is horrible. We need to stop him. You want to head to the Windy City?"

"We don't have any jurisdiction there; what do you really think you are going to do?"

"I'm going, you let the captain know that I decided to go to Chicago."

"He's going to have your ass!"

"Better than the devil having the world," he said as he uncapped the phone. "I'm on my way their Father, I've got the address on the back of your card. I'm going to stop at the police station and then I'll be right there. If you can lock down your church, I suggest that you do it as soon as you can."

"Lock it down, are you kidding me? If he knows how to kill hundreds of people do you really think a lock is going to keep him out?"

"Just be aware that he might be there, he has a few hours head start and it is impossible to say if he is going there or not. He is going to Chicago though, I have to wonder if he is headed for you?"

"I need to find Billy. Are you stopping here after you leave the Chicago Police Department?"

"I plan to keep an eye on it, unless there is something else going on. You have a partner, like this man did by chance you said?"

"Billy Parker, we've been together forever since we had to save his little brother Tony."

"Okay, well if you aren't out fighting demons, I want to meet with you. If I know where you are, I know where he will be going. If he has Intel on where you guys are going to be, then he has some kind of inside information. I don't know who would want you guys dead, I mean it, I know there are some dark ass people out there, but seriously, who wants to do something like that to someone of the cloth?"

"Someone who isn't worried about heaven, a person so dark that maybe quite literally they made a deal with Satan. That is someone that I could truly fear."

"We can talk about all this when we are face to face. You just stay alive for the next six hours and I'll be there. You think you can do that."

"I'll definitely be trying my best, Detective Dursky."

"You do that Father, you do that. Give me one less thing to regret if we live through all of this."

Chapter 19

Chicago Police Department Hours Later

Tony lay on the bench of the holding cell, he was in with everyone waiting for the processing and to be sent where they needed to go. He was mumbling in his sleep. Not one soul in the cell cared about his well-being, and those outside of it could have the same said about him. He was moaning in his sleep, the men on the bench looked at each other. The boy was skinny, sweat soaked, and his leather jacket had been removed; the vast array of different religious tattoos and crosses were hard to miss. Tony started to come around, everything he could see looked like he was trying to see it through a glass bottle. He tried to pull himself up but didn't realize the thing he was holding on to wasn't a wall but a man. When Tony felt skin beneath his sweaty fingers, he let go. A man that had two feet on Tony towered over him. He took Tony by the hand and then put his other behind his shoulder and practically threw Tony to the ground.

Tony held his hands out trying to catch himself, but with no way to see yet was unable to do anything. A voice filled with authority yelled, "Benny you leave him alone, or you are going to upset someone out here. You want out on Monday, or not?"

"Don't do much good, but mean, I don't know where my food is coming from, Boss," he said to the guard on the outside.

The guard smiled shrugging and spun on his heel walking backwards. Half the night's entertainment was watching the drunks fight it out on the inside of the cell. If they were here, nine times out of ten they deserved it and for the poor bastard that didn't, well he figured it helped them make a decision to not come back if they could possibly avoid it. The large man walked over and Tony was still trying to see. He pulled his shirt up, rubbing at his eyes with it. A pain erupted in the back of his head; the officer's, the men at the restaurant, and the people on the street came rushing back to him. The first thing he really couldn't stop thinking about was his mother and girlfriend. What would happen to them, would they know where he is, would he be getting out of here, were those things after him?

Tony screamed, the men all didn't think such a loud voice would be coming out of such a skinny young man. "Guards, hello? I need out of here, I need out of here now."

The guard on duty, Wright strolled over running his nightstick across the bars. "You aren't going anywhere until Monday, unless someone comes to bail you out. You know anyone that has enough money to bail your ass out? You'd be lucky if they charged by the pound for bail, wouldn't cost much at all."

"I'd like to call my mother and warn her."

"Warn her of what, that her son is in prison and she's going to have to go out for her own crack rock?"

"I tell you what, I have one healthy movement I need to go and take, you stay in here and keep thinking of someone that can bail you out of here. I'd love someone to post bond, the idea of having to listen to you whine for the next two days of my weekend shift doesn't do much for my sense of well-being. I already hate working weekends, I don't care to have you ruin that."

"You need to listen to me, there's something going on. Please let me call my mother, my girlfriend, or my priest."

"You need to shut up runt," Bennie said walking toward him.

Tony, not all that short himself looked up, seeing he was just barely above this man's crotch level and had to strain his neck backwards to see him. Bennie picked him up smiling, "You hear me, you little bitch? Huh, did you? You want to leave here with all your teeth and bones the way that they should be?"

Tony ignored the man screaming for the guard as he walked away. Bennie walked quickly, not affected by Tony's weight. He slammed him into the cell wall hard; the brick wall made his head pound even worse. Tony let out a lung full of breath. He squeezed his eyes shut, feeling the pain race through his skull and down his body. The man laughed and for good measure looked at the other men who started laughing to.

Tony opened his eyes slowly and saw dead eyes staring back at him. The man whispered, "The devil is everywhere boy and he got you in his sights. You were so close when you were a kid, that he thinks you could still be helpful. You let us in, you hear me?"

Tony held up his arms folding them together, he had two half crosses that made one very large one when placed together. Across them it said Cavete, Daemones in Latin meaning demons beware. The man yelled, taking a few steps back, but not letting go, his eyes went back to normal almost immediately. Tony yelled for him to let go, but the man who had him in his grasp was no happier to see him. Tony yelled for help, but the rest of the men in the cell had no reason to help him and therefore did not want to join in the pummeling, which was sure to be served. Tony looked feverishly for a guard, anyone walking by that would help him. He had never been in trouble and did not understand what was going on or why this man was doing anything to him as he had been unprovoked.

A voice that sounded like the man's when possessed came from behind him. "You should beat him, Bennie, you should rip off anything you can from him, maybe it'll teach the police to just not pick you up when you go off on a bender."

Bennie, who didn't have a handful worth of common sense nodded. He smiled and Tony could see hygiene and a lack of teeth wasn't something which bothered the man. When he went to bring Tony into the wall again, Tony brought two hands up in between the man's arms. The man didn't know what the boy was doing and Tony brought them across as hard as he could, aiming two smaller fists into the man's ears. He hit hard and the man's equilibrium immediately buckled.

Bennie let go, not wanting to, but cupping his ears was the only thing which he could think of. When he let go of Tony, he fell to the floor, he pushed back up as quickly as he could trying to right himself. Bennie took a step forward, not ready to use his hands, but for some reason worried that Tony might get away and disrespect in prison or jail was not something which was allowable.

When the man got close, Tony righted himself, bringing back a barefoot because the police took boots and shoes to give men and women one less thing to fight and kill themselves with. He unleashed it into the man's balls. Bennie tried to be ready for it, but that wasn't something that anyone could be prepared for. The pain exploded through his body and Tony took a few steps back waiting for the attack that wasn't going to come. When Bennie fell to his knees Tony took a running start jumping at just the right time to get his knee up high enough that he rammed it into the man's face. Bennie's head snapped backwards and his nose broke instantly which led to blood pouring from his face. When Bennie tried to get up, he flipped him over and kicked him once more in the ribs for good measure.

When the other man on the bench looked at Tony he saw that his eyes were not a threat, at least that of a demon possessed cell mate. Tony took a few steps backwards looking at the rest of the men in there and holding his hands ready to fight. Most of these men had seen Bennie before. This was the first time for him and they realized that they might want to treat him with a little more respect than they were thinking he originally deserved. Tony walked to the cell bars keeping an eye on the man on the ground and began screaming, drawing all the attention which he thought he needed to get some help. Unfortunately for Tony he didn't get even a look from them. When he looked behind him, he started screaming at the top of his lungs. The eyes of the cellmates started to glow red. He saw that there were a number of them that would be more than he had any chance of stopping. Tony yelled to a few of the men near him, "Do you see that, please, we need to fight them off, I need you to take care of them with me."

The men looked at who he was pointing at and figured Tony for a drunk or drug addict, not someone who was being taunted by the devil, for reasons still unknown. The man who'd been sitting on the bench stood up shoving Tony against the bars. "What is it you want us looking at you little psycho bastard. There's nothing there but a bunch of criminals. You think that there is something special about them, something that makes us different than them?"

"They are going to eat your soul; you have no idea how dark they are…how dark they can be. They are the devil's henchmen, they want all of us, they want to rule the world, to take sin to a new level."

The man laughed until the demons came running toward them. He was in between Tony and them and that was all they needed for a reason to attack him. He was not ready for the strength that the possessed had. One man single handedly lifted him by the throat with one hand spinning him around and crushing him into the bars. His skull hit first and crushed beneath the force of the impact. His echoes filled with pain consumed the ears of all to be heard which were not already taken by the demons.

Tony gripped at his chest not because of heart pain, but for his rosary and other crosses he kept. Tony was not ignorant and the fact that they had taken his belongings before they stuck him in here to live or die dawned on him quickly.

He'd made his brother Billy long ago teach him how he performs an exorcism, it had not been a quick process. Billy had told him no for weeks. When his hand fell on bare skin his stomach sank. He looked around wild-eyed. There was no shortage of criminals in the cage with him. Tony knew men like these would not be willing to put themselves before others including himself.

Tony had no clue if it would work and if it did how long it would work for but seconds extra to try and think of his next move was better than none. Tony joined his two arms in front of him, the two long black tattoos, which looked like nightsticks by themselves were united and made a foot-long solid black cross, which had the words 'Save Us, Left Not' inked in black. The demons ran toward him not veering or slowing down at all. Tony heard the keys rattling behind him feeling a moment of hope. He saw an officer frantically trying to get the door open.

"Hurry up!" Tony screamed. "Those things are almost here, get it open, now!"

Tony looked at the officer waiting to rush through, and when the sergeant looked up and met his eyes, the red glowing, no matter how light it was, was bright enough to know he was possessed as well. Tony took a big breath, springing off his foot, hoping he wouldn't get the spins again. When he heard the click of the door, he hit it with everything he had grunting in pain when his head began to throb. The door slowly started to open and Tony felt like Hulk Hogan running against Randy "The Macho Man" Savage and jumped in midair letting his feet land against the bars of the door. It slammed open hard enough that the officer flew backwards four feet, but not until the door cracked him in the skull. The demon's hands flew out and he stumbled backwards. Tony never quit running, he saw the guard's desk with a stack of envelops in a bin listed as personal belongings. He took his items and his work boots and barely stopped moving.

The guard at the desk saw the wild-eyed looking boy sprinting toward him and jumping into the air. Tony leapt over the desk right past the man as he was pulling his nightstick from its place. Tony yelled, "Get down!" but it was too late and a single bullet blew out the side of his skull.

Tony's stomach turned when the desk officer's brains and pieces of skull landed in his lap. Tony reached up blindly for the personal belongings. He realized he'd not had his wallet on him last night so when he saw a Jon Smith folder he ripped it open with his teeth wasting no time letting the contents pour into his hands. He threw the change on the floor only taking the crosses which he wore. He smiled a little, never happier before in his life to see them as right now. He took the now dead man's nightstick wrapping a crucifix around the handle. When the sixth shot from the revolver clicked and then went empty he jumped to his feet bringing back the nightstick and sending it bearing the cross directly toward the officer who'd been shooting. By now he was not the only possessed officer and Tony was aware he needed to get the hell out of dodge. The guard didn't understand what Tony was doing and he threw it with all he could muster. It struck the man in the gut making him buckle. The demon normally would not have felt a thing, but when he looked down, saw a trickle of blood. He reached for his stomach, but hit the crucifix on accident screaming in a language he didn't understand.

Tony crawled out from the side of the guard's desk, ignoring the commands from the other officers. He reached back to the guard's desk officer stealing a pair of handcuffs, unsure what he was going to use them for but seemed like a smart idea. Tony was shaking his hands trying to get the nerve he needed to run from bullets, demons, and prisoners; all who would be trying to get away. He sprinted for the doorway, not stopping for anything. Shards of wood peppered his back as he ran. The bullets were missing him by mere inches and when he was within four feet of the doorway dived into it, only coming up two feet short as he hit hard. Tony heard someone yell freeze and he scrambled to his knees the last few feet. The door was beginning to open as he approached it.

Dursky looked out the window of the plane. The flight was having massive turbulence and many people were mumbling, most looked like they were praying or if they weren't they were trying to. He always smiled at how non-believers finally found God in their final moments. He'd spent enough time in the military that shaky planes did little to make him nervous, but when a young boy yelled to his mom that the city was on fire it caught his attention. Dursky raised his privacy shade looking down seeing Chicago and even as the last hints of the sun kissed the earth goodbye, he could see that the clouds were freakish looking. The normal white, or dark was gone and replaced with clouds that resembled clouds you would expect to see in hell... given hell had clouds he thought to himself.

When a nervous stewardess walked by him, he took her by the arm. "Excuse me, can you tell me if there is something going on in Chicago? Has their tower radioed you, are we going to try and fly through that mess down there?"

She smiled, pulling his hand off gently and said, "Sir, we are turning on the seatbelt signs and we are going to do the best that we can. The pilot didn't say he'd heard any messages, but he's been flying longer than I've been alive and there is nothing he says that compares to what he is seeing now. Quite frankly, he doesn't have a damn clue what is going on. Now put that belt on and be ready to go."

Dursky nodded slowly thinking that this was not a good thing. When the plane descended, the roaring sound of the jet's engines went out. The plane felt like it was dropping in midair. There was nothing keeping it aloft soaring to the ground below. Dursky tried to look out, but all he could see were the red clouds and knew not what they meant. Dursky tried not to connect the two, but wondered if this would still be happening if he wasn't on the plane. He debated if there was something bigger going on, something unexplainable or unearthly. The stewardesses got on the intercom yelling to put your heads between their legs. Dursky sat back looking at the rest, what he saw next would only be believed by an insane person, but the red clouds parted and a blue light filled the plane. He watched and could only explain it as a cloud or a hand, something that engulfed the plane, slowing its fall. He looked to the rest of the passengers, but they were doing what they'd been asked to do.

When the blue lights faded until they were no longer there, he looked around seeing that they were on the landing strip in Chicago. His heart felt like it would explode out of his chest at any minute. Cheering came from the front and made its way throughout the entire plane. By the time things had settled down there was a definite showing of faith going on in the plane.

Dursky undid his belt not caring about the rules and pulled out a fresh pack of smokes, he tried to get one out, but when he looked at his hands he saw that they wouldn't stop shaking long enough for him to get one. The captain came over the intercom announcing that they would be departing the plane soon. Dursky who had nothing he had to carry on the plane, but what was on his person skipped ahead of the crowd showing his badge and advising it was of the utmost importance that he got off first. When he walked off the plane he'd never felt so lucky in his life.

Dursky walked through the gates until he saw an officer who was already waiting for him in the Chicago Airport. He held a picture of Dursky with directions to do what he needed to do. Dursky was carrying nothing but a folder filled with blurry images someone had been able to print from the church's security system. Dursky said, "You here for me?"

"Yes, sir, Detective Dursky, I've been told to do whatever you need, short of breaking the law."

He shook hands and said, "Point me in the right direction, officer…"

"Bohall, Sergeant Frank Bohall, or Bohall, or Franky, like he shot the bow down the hall minus the, the…well-"

"Can we go through the list of name options in the car, please? If we don't get moving, this son of a bitch is going to decide if he wants to go after another church or if he has bigger goals. Do you know if the security here was able to do anything about finding him when he got off, to verify that he did get off?"

Bohall nodded, handing him the blurry images. Dursky wasn't sure if he felt better or worse for the fact that it means he might be a dead man. He was used to running into danger, but this definitely felt like it had every bit the potential to be a million times worse.

They raced through the airport. The younger Bohall almost lost Dursky a few times. Dursky could feel his gut going up and down and this rookie was making him wonder if it was time to go on a serious new regiment…given he lived through the rest of the weekend.

✝✝✝

Dursky was having issues sitting still in the car. "So how much longer till we get to the church?"

"We aren't going to the church; my captain wants to speak to you before he lets you run around his city. Said it was important that you come in."

Dursky was going to try and think of some reason why he needed to go to the church, but he wasn't even sure where it was and knew that Bohall was more than likely his best chance of where to go and get there. When he pulled up to the front of the station, gunfire was all that could be heard. The two officers looked at each other, neither caring what they were running into.

Bohall pulled his pistol, as did Dursky. With the pew pew of bullets making their way through the metal, Dursky yelled for him to get down but heard a thud behind him. He spun while running seeing the rookie on the ground. A single blood droplet running down the center of his forehead and disappearing into his dark hairline.

"Son of a bitch!" Dursky had the hammer already pulled back and went to pull the door open and begin firing when it opened on its own. Tony came out looking half insane. He knocked into Dursky sending him backwards onto his ass, not expecting the doors to open but they did. Tony didn't ask him if he was okay. He spun around as quickly as he could pushing the doors shut and attaching a pair of oversized handcuff chains through the door handles praying that he wouldn't be the next bullet wound victim. Tony clicked them tight and ran down to the fallen officer removing his nightstick and sprinted, jamming it into the spot and wrapping the extra chain with it.

"We gotta go!" Tony screamed, trying to put a hand on Dursky.

Dursky slipped to the side gripping onto Tony's arm and throwing him to the ground safe out of the way of the possessed who were currently sending lead through the door as quickly as they could. "Who the hell are you, what is going on inside of there?" Dursky yelled in about the most authoritative voice Tony had ever heard.

"You'll think I'm insane, if I tell you. Tell you what, how bout we get out of here first before we get killed."

"I'm a cop they aren't going to-"

The door exploded open before the two of them could finish talking. Three police and two criminals each had a pistol and were aiming directly for the two of them. Dursky pulled Tony back to his feet dragging him behind. Dursky looked over his shoulder, seeing confidently that some of the men with guns shouldn't have them; the men who should have them were pointing them at a fellow officer. It didn't take two looks to know Dursky had been on the job for decades but what stood out more than anything was the five men's eyes. They practically burned like embers, and when the doors shut as they stepped out of their way, they seemed to glow even brighter.

Dursky didn't wait any longer because they aimed and the five started firing the pistols. Tony thought about them knowing that the crosses would not protect the two of them from bullets screaming across the pavement toward them. Dursky screamed in agony when a bullet tore through his thigh. Tony saw him going down toward the ground. He leapt forward ducking low, almost duck walking for a moment and got under him before he could completely fall to the ground. Dursky wrapped his arm around Tony's shoulder. Tony wasn't ignorant and knew that they'd not be going far. The two of them made it to Bohall's squad car and he dumped him into the passenger seat. He slammed the door shut just as bullets dug their way into the door.

Dursky screamed again as Tony had to put his weight on his leg by accident to make his way into the driver's seat. "I'm sorry, are you going to be okay, are you all right?"

Tony looked over to him seeing his eyes looking a bit red, until he saw it was from the traffic lights in front of them. Tony took one of the thicker crosses and slid it over Dursky's head without asking. "You keep that, you keep that on you."

"I need a doctor you little shit, not a cross!"

"They can take you, you might not want them to, you could fight, but trust me, once they get their claws on your soul there's nothing you can do."

Dursky pushed up out of his seat, but immediately ducked back down. Tony did his best to keep it straight, bullets riddled the back of the car. The glass in the rear of the car shattered. Dursky undid his belt ripping it off and put it around his thigh. From the pain that was burning in his leg he could tell the bullet had entered and exited. "What in the hell was wrong with those people, why were they shooting. I need some goddamn answers before I lose my mind!"

"I don't have any answers that are gonna make any sense. My name's Tony, Tony Parker. I- "

"Parker, your last name is Parker. You got a brother by chance that wears the cloth?"

Tony looked over not too sure of what to say or how this guy knew anything about his brother. He saw the badge on his neck and the bold embossed gold letters he had seen in movies shown across it LAPD. "You aren't from Chicago? Who the hell are you and why are you talking about my brother, what do you want?"

"Hopefully to save his life, kid."

"From what, you didn't have a cross on, you aren't in with the church."

"Look, get me to a doctor first, would ya? This isn't going to heal itself and I need it stitched up, and a shot of painkillers wouldn't break my heart."

Tony nodded hitting the gas and Dursky flipped the lights giving him a straight shot to the all night medical clinic. Tony drove right up to the front laying on the horn. The clinic wasn't a stranger to gunshot wounds and within seconds a large black man was running toward the car with a wheelchair which had a long piece of duct tape going up the middle of it. Dursky looked at the state of the chair and then the building and said, "You are telling me this is the best thing that they've got in town?"

"Best thing we are going to make it to. The last thing you probably want to do is bleed while I drive across town, right?"

Dursky debated this and nodded. "Thanks for driving kid, I'm not going to lie, I'm feeling a little light-headed. You think you can get me in there?"

The door opened and the man looked at Dursky and his eyes. He ducked beneath the steel doorframe getting Dursky under the armpits. When his hand touched beneath his thigh he came right back around screaming at the top of his lungs. Tony saw the look of pain and knew he wasn't messing around. He set him much gentler into the wheelchair and the two disappeared. Tony parked the car and found Dursky by his yells echoing down the hall. He felt a sense of relief as he walked down room by room and a plethora of crosses and religious relics were everywhere. When he found the room he was in he disappeared, finding the hospital's chapel and took a cup from a water dispenser and found the holy water. He scooped up a cup and sprinted to the main entrance dipping his fingers into the water and making a cross on it. He ran a line across the front and ran fingers down the edges. Nurses were looking at the young man thinking he looked like a lunatic. Tony wanted to explain, but much like the detective, didn't think that they would believe him until they had seen the hell in a demon's eyes.

Tony ran back to the room hoping that it would be enough, that they would survive and they'd be gone and not leave any reasons for the demons to come into the room. When he ran around the man who'd wheeled him in, he was holding him down. Dursky had a belt in his mouth and at first, thought that the doctor and orderly had been possessed, but upon getting closer saw that Dursky looked like the crazy one. "Would you hold him down please, he has the strength of a crack head!"

The orderly practically lay atop of Dursky to keep him down. When he had him still the doctor brought out a needle and put it in his leg just above the wound as gently as he could. Dursky spit the belt out yelling, "I hate freaking needles, get that thing out of my leg!"

The orderly looked at Tony and even with his huge size was still unable to keep him on the table properly. The doctor said, "There, we are done, can you relax now, god damn? I've met people who don't appreciate needles, but this son of a bitch takes the freaking win. Good lord, I thought he was going to kill himself on that needle. All we were trying to do, sir, was keep your leg from getting infected. I've never seen someone fight that hard. Now sit still, I just need to stitch it and wrap it and you can get checked in after that."

Tony said, "Does he need to stay here overnight, doc?"

"He should, but I have a suspicion that he isn't smart enough to listen to doctor's orders."

Dursky wiped at the spit on his mouth. "You don't understand what is going on. If you can just get me back into a wheelchair after you fix me up, we will be good."

"What do I know, I only have a decade of schooling and then doing this under my belt, what would I know. You want to bust through those stitches you be my guest. I frankly don't give a damn."

"I just need to make it through tonight, and I'll come back and let you stick all the needles that you want in me. You think you can do that?"

"Whatever you say chief."

Within ten minutes the doctor had his leg stitched close. Dursky was waiting impatiently, but the man took his time making sure it would stay closed. He wrapped it as tight as he could with bandages and Dursky was already half way off the table when Tony said, "You uh forgetting something?"

Dursky looked down at his Spiderman boxers and realized quickly he didn't have any pants on. The orderly laughed lightly. "When you passed out, I cut them off. You want a pair of scrubs, or you want to go look in lost and found? I wouldn't suggest the latter if you don't want bed bugs or head lice though."

Dursky pointed to the scrubs the man had on. The orderly was back in a few minutes with a pair of green pants that Tony and he held up for Dursky to slide into. Dursky had beads of sweat populating his forehead. "Where's your brother kid?"

Tony looked at the clock, he didn't keep tabs on Billy and knew that if there were demons to send to hell he'd be out fighting them. "We can go by the church, or if you promise not to run off I'll go check on him. You think you can sit here for two minutes while I check on it?"

Dursky motioned for him to leave and the orderly helped him get his bad leg back up on the bed. Dursky laid back ready to pass out, but shook his head, trying to keep in the game. "You hurry up!"

Tony disappeared out of the room, the fact that his girlfriend had been left at work and his mom unaccounted for as of when he went to jail made him sick to his stomach. Within a half hour the two were headed out, disobeying every order the doctor had told him, but with an influx of patients coming with gunshot wounds realized that there were more important things to be done. Tony had poked his head out of the doorway, hearing a few police in the hallway talking about how the precinct where Tony had been was on some sort of drugs and everyone had lost their minds. The civilians walking in the streets had been gunned down, something Tony instantly felt guilty about, even though he knew that there was nothing he could do. He was somewhat surprised they had not tried to take the bodies, unless Satan had been trying to send demons to heaven again, he questioned.

Dursky whistled until he couldn't stand it and began cursing when his leg muscles contracted as he got out of the hospital bed. He looked at the cheap metal cane the doctor had given him with the advice to put as little weight on it as possible and thought the odds were stacked against them, of course, had he known who the real players were tonight and that Satan was leading the way he would have been even less optimistic.

Chapter 20

Billy checked his watch. He felt like his heart was going to explode. He felt light-headed as his pulse was racing and therefore was making his hand want to explode. It had quit bleeding for a while, but had just squeezed the handkerchief tighter in his hand. He was halfway to the church when he realized he needed to know his family was okay.

He changed direction running for his mother's house. The thought that even one demon let alone an entire horde of them were after Tony again, made him sick. He tried to think of the times he'd fought them and realized he was on his own, and had no backup, no way to get hold of James or Father Michaels and didn't know if they were even at the church to call. He wasn't thinking practically and wanted to find his mother and Tony in hopes that he could do something to save them or if they were safe still, move them into the church and its protection.

He was determined and fearful and he didn't take long to make it to his mom's. He tried to watch every person as he sprinted looking like a crazy man in the streets. Billy didn't focus on what they were carrying, how they were standing, he watched their eyes waiting for them to suddenly turn red. The last thing he wanted to see were five hundred sets of red eyes chasing him down. He thought of the zombies in the street knowing that they were still somewhere, unsure what they were going to do with them. Billy tried to think of what the plan was, what they were doing and could come up with nothing. He was confident that there was something much bigger at play here, but the end game was hard to see.

When Billy made it to the doorstep, he could see lights on already. He did the sign of the cross with a short prayer that everything he'd been worrying for on the way here was where it should be. He knew if he had to run all over town looking for Tony that it could be too late by the time that he found him. He didn't knock and used his key to get in. His mother was reading at the table and there were no worries, at least...not yet on her face. Billy was sure that he was about to ruin that.

Joan looked up to see him, smiling until her motherly instincts took over and she did what every mother did and that was do a run over his personal appearance. His suit was dirty and torn from the exorcism earlier, his hand covered with a handkerchief and by now was fully soaked through with blood, his face swollen, scraped, and more than likely had dry blood. Small drops were finding their way to the ground and it was the only noise in the house. "Where's Tony, mom, I need to find him."

"Tony, what happened, Billy?"

"Mom, I don't have time for-"

"Don't you mom me, William Parker, not for one damn minute. You tell me what is wrong with you, why you are standing in my living room bleeding and you look like you went to hell and back?"

Billy held up his hand, seeing it and how the running had not helped keep it from bleeding worse. He went to the kitchen sink, pulling the handkerchief off, wincing when he did. "Look, it isn't as bad as it seems. James and I had a job today, I don't think that I need to tell you what kind of job it was. It didn't go well-"

"Oh, Billy, honey, are you okay, I mean, did you save whomever it was that needed helping, who you were trying to save?"

"Yeah, we saved them, I almost lost James in the process but we came through. If it wasn't for that whole God thing and being able to help more than other people because we knew that he was there and there was a real fight I like to think maybe being an accountant sounds nice. I can't think punching a calculator is all that hard, I was always good at math."

"Do you remember your report cards? I don't think it would have been an option for you dear. So why are you looking for Tony, what is going on?"

"I just want to make sure that he's okay. The demon said something about him, about the family and how they wanted him back. It didn't set well with me and I want to get him to the church. I want you there too, until this is over. I can call your boss and explain, or whatever you want to do, you tell me. But I want to get a bag for the two of you, and I want to get out of here. I don't like the way the city is acting, it seems off to me, I don't know how to explain it."

"A priest who is freaked out about demons is all that I need. If you think that things are worse than normal, the last thing I want to do is sit and argue with you. I just hope it isn't like all those years ago."

Billy nodded; he had no issues remembering what it was that happened all those years ago. "I pray that it isn't that serious, but with all the work I've done, all the people whom I've saved, there has never been a demon who has taunted me threatening my family. I don't know what they want with him or you for that matter, but I'm sure as hell not going to do anything that is going to jeopardize the two of you. Go get a bag and come on, we need to go and find Tony, else I'll drop you off at the church get James and the two of us can go together."

"Oh, wouldn't that be just lovely, leave me with a nun or Father Michaels to worry sick over the lot of you. Can we please do that?" Joan said hands on her hips and full of sarcasm.

"Would you rather have a demon rip you in half and make Tony and I have to look at our only mother in the world lying on the ground with her gut-"

"Christ our Lord, would you quit! You are going to make me see things that I am unable to forget. Take a breath Billy, let's get a couple things and head out."

She went up the stairs with Billy behind her, he told her to go get her clothes, enough for a few days and some toiletries for the two of them and he'd only be a few minutes. Billy went into Tony's room, the same one the two of them had shared for almost two decades together. His posters from boyhood long gone. The cross that had burned off the wall as children now replaced many, many times over. Those who had been allowed to know about the demons had happily bought the boys crosses every time they'd seen one. At one point, they finally had to start turning them down, as they had no more room with which to hang them.

Billy opened the dresser seeing nothing but a pack of smokes, a Bible and a backup rosary bead necklace. He went through the rest of the drawers not seeing any clothes. He could only shake his head at his brother being a slob. He could already imagine finding all of his work overalls crumpled on the ground and a selection of equally messy looking Levi's and black pocket T-shirts lying with it. He looked under the bed, finding a backpack and opened the door to the closet. Had he known what he was getting himself into he would not have laid a finger on the knob.

The demons practically barked with laughter when he broke the holy barrier and the door knob ripped from his grasp. Billy looked at his hand, seeing welts that could very well be blisters soon forming on the inside of his palm. The force of the demons sent him back five feet on to Tony's bed. He hit with a bounce already swinging his momentum, ignoring the pain and rushing toward the hallway door. It slammed shut before he could reach it and Billy ran with everything he had. He looked behind him and while he could not see it, he knew that there was something evil in the room. He knew they wouldn't take him but would sure as hell toss him out of the window with great satisfaction. Billy ran straight into the door. The force with which he hit it with sent it off the hinges shattering the wood frame.

Billy stumbled out falling on the broken door. His mother, Joan had jumped three feet, clasping her chest, frightened that her heart might come out of it and tossed the bag full of toiletries in the air spilling them everywhere. Billy could feel something go past him and when he looked back at his mother who had been dressed to be in for the night noticed she did not have her cross on. He realized she'd either taken it off or it had come off when she changed. He screamed to her, but knew it would be too late if he didn't do something. "Ma, get in the tub, get in the tub and turn on the water, do it now, do it, plug the drain!"

It took a minute for Joan to realize what she was hearing because it made no damn sense at all. She climbed into the tub carefully not caring or needing to take off any clothes. She watched the look of fright in Billy's eyes and feared for her own safety as she watched the frames along the short hallway begin to shake frantically. She put in the stopper turning the water on full blast. The echoes of pain filled the hallway.

Billy kicked off of the door until he was back on the wood floor. He rushed down it seeing the door beginning to shake. He knew that if it shut, that she would either be taken by them or they would try and send her to hell by making her break some Catholic commandment. Billy got a few balls full of holy water from his pocket, feeling around and seeing that yes, there was very little left of them in his pocket. He took out three of them diving for the bathroom and throwing the glass against the white plastic of the bathtub. They thankfully shattered against it and the holy water mixed with the bath and formed a shield for Joan. He cringed when the radio began to float across the floor toward her and still plugged in. The digital numbers blinking six six six on them. Billy ran sliding and threw one last ball shattering it and it fell to the floor breaking into pieces.

The screams of frustration and failure came back toward Billy. They lifted him off his feet dragging him backwards at speeds he did not know that demons could travel. They tossed him up in the air. Billy had lived there long enough to know the hallway wasn't long and didn't need to look to know he was almost out of the hallway. At the end of it was a staircase and a balcony and neither of those were something he wanted to deal with falling down.

The invisible hands let go, he felt nothing beneath him now but gravity and air. Billy held out his hand, the best one he had to use now given the nail wound in the other. His hand hit against the railing and he used everything he could to grasp on and clench his fingers around it. Billy felt thankful when he could feel the wood beneath his grasp, at least until his momentum stopped and he jerked to a stop almost letting go. His body stopped moving in the direction and he swung down, hitting hard against the side steps. He tried to pull himself up but between a burnt hand and the other with a nail wound through it could barely believe that he was able to hold on this long. His grasp slipped and he fell from the balcony to the ledge beneath it.

He heard the house's front door rattling, realizing something was either trying to get out or in, but wasn't sure what. A thin hand weathered from age and years of manual labor wrapped around his wrist followed by the other. Joan smiled, soaking wet sitting on the edge of the step pulling with everything she could muster to try and get her oldest son a helping hand. She helped give him the time and reassurance that she could and when Billy had an elbow under him, he was able to pull the rest of his weight up. When he made it over the edge of the steps the door burst open. Billy saw Dursky come through gun up and running...or doing his best to hobble.

Dursky came off like a crazy man with a dirty work shirt and tie, a pair of green scrub pants and a large pistol in his hand aiming it where he looked. Billy scrambled to his feet pushing his mother in front of him as they headed back down the hallway. When they passed the hall closet he opened it getting a baseball bat he still kept at the house as his quarters in the church were not plentiful. He ran the best he could for the stairs. Dursky was coming up the steps as fast as he could, he had not seen Billy coming yet and when he was within a few feet could just barely duck in time to not have Billy take his head off with the slugger. Billy yelled, "Get out of my house demon, your body will be no good to you once I knock the head off it!"

Dursky fell backwards as he avoided the massive swing. Even with Billy's bum hands, he still swung the bat with a hate filled angst. Dursky let go of the cane using his hand to grip onto the banister. Billy had wasted no time getting ready with a second swing, but Tony was at the bottom of the steps screaming at the top of his lungs. "Billy, he's here to help, he's here to help, don't do it!"

Billy shook his head, making sure that he wasn't seeing things. He knew the demons could get inside your head and wasn't about to let him be fooled?"

"Anthony, is that you?"

"Only mom gets to call me that ass and you know it!"

Billy let the bat down slowly smiling, nodding his head. "Yeah, that's you, who the hell is this, and why didn't you come in first?"

"I was parking the car, he took a shot to the leg earlier. He helped me get out of jail."

Joan, who was a mom above all else yelled, "What do you mean you were in jail, Anthony Parker?"

"It wasn't my fault, MA!"

"You accidentally ended up in jail?" Asked Billy

"There were demons, they were taking people over in plain sight. I was the only one that saw them of course. I bolted from there, two cops stopped me...probably for looking like an insane man. I woke up in a cell after one of them clubbed me over the head. It didn't take long before whatever had been on the outside started coming after me in the cell. One of the guards opened the door and I kicked it and got out. By the time I was halfway through the door guns started going off and they were coming for me. When I made it outside they weren't far behind me. Dursky took one in the leg and I took him to the hospital. I wanted to make sure mom was okay, I was going to take her to the church. I figured you were going to be okay on your own as long as you had James' help."

Billy walked down the stairs with his mother in hand. When he got close enough to Dursky to see the LAPD on his shield he pointed at it. "So, what the hell are you doing here in Chicago, sir? Don't get me wrong, I'm very appreciative that you saved my baby brother, but what are you doing out here?"

"I was in LA this morning, minding my own business. I got a call about a homicide with a maid. Things I won't dare repeat. Not much later there was a call about deaths at a church, massive numbers of deaths, the type that you only see when an entire congregation decide to try and move on to the next step in life and think that they are above Earth."

"It was a Catholic Church? How does that tie in with the maid, if you don't mind me asking, Detective?"

"Just call me Dursky, the maid was...are you sure you want to hear this, ma'am we don't have to..."

Joan smiled, still dripping wet with holy water and shaking her head. "You think that you are going to scare me, I assure you that you have no idea the things I've seen. I'd happily trade you with what my old eyes have lay witness to."

"She was crucified onto the hotel's wall. The two that saw the man who was in the room that morning said he was dressed like a priest, that is the connection to the church, not saying anyone can't just dress up but when we checked the video all we got were blurry face images. When we went to the church we saw the same thing, and the men that were at the airport who got information from their video feed for me saw the exact same thing. I don't know what kind of tricks he's using but it seems like it has something to do with his face. I really can't say."

Billy nodded, trying to think about it attempting to put everything in order in his head. "You said a congregation, there were priests there, they had priests that...what were their names?"

Dursky flipped open his thin manila folder. He saw the two names, and read them off like they wouldn't mean anything to anyone else. His job as a homicide detective felt more like at times he was just going through the motions. He didn't give up, he didn't hate the job, but he did not try to think of the victims as people. They were facts, they were statistics but they weren't someone that could come into his dreams. "There was a Father Edwards and a Father Nathaniel."

The words hit like an uppercut. He stumbled back a few feet losing his breath and falling onto the steps and sat down taking a second. "Did you know them, Billy?" Joan asked, concern in her voice. The idea that someone might one day come to her doorstep to deliver bad news like this wasn't something she let herself think about regularly, but enough that she had lost sleep because of it.

"Yes, Father Nathaniel was only a few years older than us, he was one of two in charge of exorcisms in that region. We didn't deal with Father Edwards all that much. What about Father Carter, did he make it?"

"Other than some kids and ex-alcoholics there weren't any survivors. I don't have any reports on him, but didn't have any reason to check. I'm sure that the rest of the parish had been accounted for."

"I can check with James when we get to the church. You said you were parking the car, you good with giving us a ride, Dursky?"

"Sure, I say the sooner we make sure the two of you are safe the better. Do you know why anyone might have done that, why he might have been killed?"

"I don't have a clue why, people are weird, some are just evil, they never found the way into church. Other than a few times when we went out to California to teach them, we didn't really know them, never really had a lot of reasons to go talk to them. We helped train them and supplied them with some of our tools of the trade. The kind of things they didn't have back before the two of us got taken on to do this work. We had Father Michaels and he was our biggest supporter. No idea was too small or big if it would help. As we got going when we started, we got more and more things out and...none of this matters it won't change anything. Let's just hope that they found their way to heaven."

"We need to get to the church. I can only assume that you guys are the only ones doing this in Chicago, right?" Dursky asked.

"Yes, sir, we take care of most of the Midwest and anywhere that needs any help."

"How many other priests are there that we need to worry about?"

"I'd have to count, but I'd say sixteen, twenty tops? Some are still in training. This doesn't happen overnight. Becoming a priest isn't a quick thing, sir."

"Does someone you know have a list?"

"Father Michaels oversees everyone. He spends a great deal of time travelling, more when things are acting up. When we get to the church he'll have numbers and we can reach anyone on that list. You obviously feel this guy is going to be coming after us, those priests with a specialized mission in life?"

Tony said, "You guys do realize that this is all shit we could be saying in the car, you know on the way there? Like where the church is, and where we could be verifying all this stuff and seeing if the California guys were the first on the list or if you guys are the last of it. Maybe he made more things look like accidents, or big things that…"

"We need to leave then," Joan said. When no one moved, she screamed, "Now, we need to get to James!"

Billy smiled, Tony and himself were by far her favorite things on earth but if he had a third it would be James. She knew all the times when her husband was still around and food was scarce that Billy would pass on his portions to Tony and would find his food elsewhere. James had been the one who helped make sure his best friend didn't starve. James of course and his family. The last thing they could do was let that pass.

The four of them left through the front. When they opened the door, a crowd was filling the street. They were blocking the exit to the car, blocking their exit to anywhere. Dursky held his shield in one hand, and his revolver in the other. Billy took his wrist gently and lowered it. "You don't have enough bullets, put it down."

"We can't quit!" Dursky yelled, the veins in his forehead were visibly pulsating from the circumstances.

Billy said it as slowly and as calmly as if he was asking to pass the salt. "Look at their eyes, you could put up every round you have in one of them and they are just gonna keep coming, smiling and running."

"You don't have a prayer, something you can do to get those things out of them?"

"I don't think you understand what a priest has got to do, what they go through to be able to save a life from one of these. It is as much mental as it is physical," Tony tried to explain.

"So, you can't Jesus our way out and I can't shoot them? You aren't leaving too many options here that are overly desirable," Dursky yelled punching the door in frustration.

Billy, who was already frustrated by about everything he'd had to face throughout his day yelled, "I can't Jesus my way out of this, good God Almighty, please save me from this... this-"

"Watch what you say priest, I'm a bad catholic, and I'd think even God would give me a pass right now," Dursky said as he puffed up his chest.

Billy looked to Dursky thinking it had been a long time since he was ready to deck someone, even if it was someone who had come for a good reason. He knew that he wasn't necessarily trying to save James' and his lives so much as catch the guy who is taking all of them. When he saw Tony's lip quivering, he was unsure what to expect that he would see. Billy gasped when he made eye contact, or at least what he could only call eye contact since he could see through the thing in front of them. Dursky and Joan could not see it and Billy was fine with that because it'd just be one more thing to waste time about. Tony took Billy's shoulder trying not to sound insane. "You...you see it too, right, Billy? You see it, tell me you do, please, I feel like after today I'm starting to lose my damn mind."

Billy nodded and it didn't take long to see the young man in front of him or who the young spirit of the ghost had been. "Father Joseph, is that you? Is that really you?"

Joseph hovered forward. "You can put the holy water away, Billy, I'm on your side. The powers that be thought that you might need a push tonight to help you make it through the evening. It is good to see you again, it has been too long."

"You look; you look so much different, what in the world happened after you died?"

"Not everyone keeps their form, some of us are resulted back to how we were better remembered. I just happened to be in my thirties, probably not too much older than you arc now."

Tony, who had not realized who he was until he began speaking said, "You said you were sent? Who sent you, are you going to be able to help us?"

"I don't think we need to answer that," Joseph replied quietly.

Dursky and Joan both exchanged glances seeing if either of them could see what it was in front of them. When they both concluded that they couldn't see whatever it was they just looked at Tony and Billy, who were having a conversation as plain as day. "You want to let us know what the plan is, Billy, since you obviously aren't going to tell your mother any of the important information."

"We don't know yet, mom," Billy replied.

She nodded her head slowly watching as the front door began to rattle. Tony said, "Doesn't look like we get to be privy to what is happening as well. You think he's going to be able to do it?" Tony asked.

"If not, I can't think of anything else that he has up there that is going to be able to help us," Billy replied.

The four walked to the window prying it open. The heavy wooden door opened and stayed open after he left. Tony said, "I think he wants us to go with him."

"Why do you say that?" Joan said after hearing the two of them.

"Because he's sitting out there waving after us, I don't know where he is going, but I think he wants us to follow," Tony replied.

Billy took his mom by the hand and Tony walked out side by side with Dursky. When they made it outside there was a path that was opening. The demons that had taken over the humans seemed to know what was happening or at least what the consequences were if they crossed the path. When the four of them were close to the inner circle the two boys watched as Joseph quit moving forward. A light that Billy and his mother had only experienced once before slowly started to grow, no larger than the size of a softball. The two of them watched it, remembering it almost knocking down the house when they had seen it before.

Billy pulled her close, holding her hand and saying prayers beneath his breath. Tony heard what he was saying and needed no help recollecting what he was reciting. He took his mother's other hand and Dursky who tried to pull him away at first but Tony only gripped tighter. The blue light practically exploded onto the ground and across the streets until it disappeared from sight. They squinted their eyes shut, not wanting to worry about going blind. When they opened their eyes, the demons were no longer in control of the bodies. People now no longer possessed were tossed everywhere like rag dolls. Joan saw it and pulled both of her sons off balance, making Tony let go of Dursky and squeezed the two of them. Billy was looking everywhere for Joseph but he could be found nowhere. He looked to the sky just in time to see the bluest blue he'd ever seen before it disappeared into a twinkle.

Dursky cleared his throat, looking around at the people now. "What in the hell just happened?"

The two brothers both shrugged. "I don't think they wanted anyone else to know this time."

"Oh, of course, because it has happened before?" Dursky inquired jokingly.

"Pretty much," Tony said, not wasting any time and began to walk toward the squad car. "These things look free right now but who knows how long it's going to last like this. These people might only be safe for so long. We need to secure the vehicle, get out of here and to James and Father Michaels."

Billy held his mother tight knowing at this time they could not be more vulnerable. That someone above had saved them and for that he was thankful. Tony revved the engine and they peeled out, leaving a trail of smoke and the newly saved in their wake.

Dursky was trying his best to light a smoke but couldn't do it. Tony motioned for the lighter using it on a smoke which he passed to Dursky and then one for himself. His mother cleared her throat never being a big fan of smokers or the waste of money on the habit. Tony looked in the rearview shaking his head. "A city full of the dead and the possessed and you still gotta bust me down for trying to smoke, MA?"

"I'm your mother, Anthony, and I can do and say as I please! You don't forget that."

Billy snickered in the backseat and his mother gave him a bump with her elbow. "Even God won't save you from me if you don't show a little respect, William Parker."

Billy knew better than to talk back to her and they sped toward the church. The graveyards they passed by in the city could just barely be seen but they could tell there was a presence in them and they were beginning to be overrun by the dead. Billy said, "I hope there's a plan to take care of these things, we can't be greedy but there's only so much we can handle."

Dursky had the smoke hanging only by dried spit and the red ember of the end was only a finger width away from burning his chin. Tony looked over at him laughing, "You said that you'd seen about everything, right? Well, this is probably something new to you, huh?"

Dursky grabbed at his smoke when he could feel the heat on his chin. He looked back to Billy and yelled, "What in the hell do you plan on doing with all those things? How the hell are they out of the ground?"

"You ever hear how God works in mysterious ways? Well, so does the devil, apparently. As far as what we are going to do we need to get these two to the church and make sure that James and Father Michaels are all right. After that we will regroup and come up with a-"

"Shit!" Tony screamed. He slammed down hard on the brakes with no worry for anyone's safety as he spun the wheel around the corner. "I forgot that Alecia was working. We got to go get her, like now!"

"We don't have time to go get your girlfriend, Tony," Dursky said.

"Would you go after your family? I bet that you would. She doesn't have much and I'm not going to have her in the streets on a night like this one. Who knows what she is dealing with or what is going on over on that side of town."

Dursky wanted to say something but he didn't know anyone here well enough to say anything. When they made it to the restaurant they could see that there had to be a serious graveyard near them because the dead populated everything. Tony was grateful for the dead versus the possessed. In his mindset he thought they were better off because he wasn't sure that he could allow himself to run into someone knowing the damned might leap out of them in time to let them absorb the pain.

He wanted to stop out front but could see already that there were too many of the dead to do so. He went racing around the corner, down the street picking off the dead that were in his way. Brittle bones smashed from the impact covering the hood with limbs and skulls still snapping their jaws. The two both tossed their smokes when the clicking noise got even louder. Tony raced down the alley hoping that they would not have made it there yet. When they saw it empty they both felt there was something at work here looking out for him.

When Tony slid to a stop in front of the back door, he left the car going and he and Billy both slid out of the car not having to ask him to go with to save Alecia. When they headed into the kitchen Alecia was there standing on a table along with a cook and a bus boy, each of them holding brooms and mops trying to keep the dead at bay. When Tony entered the room, he could see there was no shortage of the dead that had made their way in. Tony looked to Billy, who was trying to figure out how to deal with this.

"Alecia, hey baby, we are going to save you, you just stay there!" Tony asked.
Alecia looked at him with hope which immediately turned to annoyance at the fact that he had to tell the three of them to stay there, as if there was a choice. The young cook was kicking at them, not paying attention to his surroundings and knocked over a cup of water. When he lifted his right foot to kick at one of the dead, he lost his

balance and slipped hard onto his back grunting when he did. The dead, wasted no time gripping him by the white shirt and pants and dragged him from the table to the ground.

The man screamed as the first of ten mouths took hold onto his legs and arms and began tearing viciously, painfully, and fatally at his body. Alecia bent to try and do something but was pulled back up by the young bus boy. Tears were streaming freely from Alecia, the visual she had was an up close and personal horror show.

Billy wouldn't allow another soul to be taken, but knew his supplies were low and there were too many of the dead for him to be able to handle on his own. He patted at his pockets, there were only three balls left filled with holy water. He ran into the back where they'd entered to the sink. Tony watched, baffled that he'd just abandoned him to figure out a way on his own to get Alecia. He looked around the diner trying to see what he could use for a weapon but was thinking there wasn't anything to use. He looked behind the counter, smiling when he saw a sawed-off shotgun. Tony checked to see what was in it, and barely had any idea how to use it. Firing it off toward his girlfriend didn't seem like a very intelligent idea.

He turned it around ready to use it as a baseball bat as his brother came running back with a bucket of water in each hand. He broke the two pieces of glass together over the buckets trying to let as much of the water spill as possible into the already full buckets. Billy smiled at Tony doing the sign of the cross and wincing as he picked the bucket up. Billy brought it back and then spun with it launching the water from the bucket into the air in an arc. He stood there not worried about the second bucket until he could see the effects of the first. They held their breath as they watched the water make contact with the dead. Smoke rose from their bones, and on some who had not been in the ground for long and only had a pale complexion with minimal holes in their skin from the bugs, it began to sizzle. The smell was already horrific, but when it made its way through it made everything smell fifty times worse.

Tony saw that it worked and bent down looking like a running back, a sport he'd only ever had time to admire and ran, not waiting for Billy.

Billy looked at Tony watching him race toward the dead that were now dripping wet with makeshift holy water. He kept his arms up in front of him, knocking the dead out of the way with each step, the muscles in his legs burned as he pushed them from his path, stopping for nothing. Alecia looked even more worried and the dead gripped onto his arms when he made it up to them. A mouth was coming straight for his neck, the teeth clicking as it got closer and closer. He tried to pull his arm free from its grip but couldn't free himself. Tony head-butted it before it could bite him but it could not feel pain and all he did was bruise his forehead. He was thinking of his favorite prayer, waiting for the pain to come. When it didn't he opened his eyes to see that the bus boy had jammed his broom handle into its mouth. Tony smiled, only temporarily relieved as another of the dead was ready to finish what the other had begun. When the mouth was only inches away he screamed in rage, frustrated with the circumstances; that was when a bath of water splashed across the back of his neck and hair drenching him and the dead in front of him.

Billy ran up holding out a hand to help Alecia and the boy down off the table. Billy elbowed him yelling, "Come on and get them to the back, we gotta go!"

Tony didn't waste time but couldn't help himself, his emotions were racing wild from adrenaline. He gripped his brother practically breaking his back when he clenched onto him, squeezing him in a bear hug. "How did you know that was going to work?"

Billy let out some air, trying to squeeze back but his hands were almost shot and in need of some very serious medical attention. "I had absolutely no idea if it would work or not but it was the only thing I had going for me as an option."

Alecia cleared her throat, "Hey, Tony, are we getting out of here or not?"

Tony let go quickly of Billy holding up his outstretched arms to his girlfriend. She practically leapt into them and he gracefully took hold of her, setting her down being careful of the holy water. The bus boy got down as well and the four made their way back to the car wasting no time. Joan smiled when she saw Alecia safe and sound, knowing if Tony never made it into the priesthood as he wished that he would at the very least have a woman that was good by his side and would care for him and give her the grandbabies that would fill her own life with joy.

Tony opened the door, Billy and the bus boy both slid into the back. Alecia into the front with Dursky waiting behind the wheel and Tony slammed the door as he punched the gas. Dursky smiled, running the engine at screaming decibels. "Now that we got your girlfriend can we get to the church?"

Tony's relief and joy felt like it had been lessened for the simple fact that he had knowingly put the life of others after that of his girlfriend's. He tried to think and rationalize with himself why it was okay to do that and if it was something that meant he truly didn't need to be a member of the church, given that he lived through the night.

They sped with Dursky looking around trying to make his way through the town. The dead were beginning to be a nuisance, each of them dressed from a different decade it seemed and then to have them stumbling arms out and mouth clicking in the street. He'd been hesitant the first few, trying his best to respect the dead but it grew old quick and any of them in front were taken out.

When they were within a block of the church they had to stop the car. The dead were everywhere, with demons in front of the church. It was quite literally hell on earth. Billy leaned in between Tony and Alecia peering at the numbers in front of them. The holy water he had in his pockets wasn't enough to make a dent in this. Tony saw Billy trying to figure things out and asked, "So what do you wanna do, Billy? I don't think we have enough of anything to help out."

"You are the demon killer right or whatever it is, you send these things back to hell, you know where they belong?" Dursky asked.

The bus boy cleared his throat asking, "Is there a reason that you brought me here? I don't think this is any better than what was at the restaurant. I didn't think I could feel any worse but you-"

Billy opened the door, letting the boy out. He quit midsentence sprinting off into the night, never happier than to be out of work and away from a church in all his life. The small group watched as his white uniform disappeared into the darkness. Tony said, "What if we go down through the tunnel? Is there a way to get into the church from there, were there contingency plans put in place when that thing was built?"

"I don't think there'd been any reason to have any secret tunnels put in place. The front is the only way to get in," Billy said reluctantly.

Billy put his head down, pulling out his rosary beads, praying that there was something the man upstairs could do for him. It would not take much to make him even more thankful than he'd already been. He thought back to how God had sent all these things back to hell once tonight and wondered if there'd be another opportunity to see him flex his almighty power. A voice whispered after a few minutes of praying. He could feel a hand on his shoulder, one that made all his pain temporarily go away along with his fear and worries. When he opened his eyes, he saw the two priests that had helped him as a boy. One was Father Joseph who'd been alive at the time and the other who'd been for lack of a better word a ghost or spirit, Father Andrew. Billy smiled, watching the blue light float from their outlines, he could see through them to the outside. "Father Joseph, I need your help, more than you could imagine!"

The man's face lightened as he smiled, nodding, saying nothing. Father Andrew and Joseph walked into the street. Billy looked to the others to see if they were able to see what he was and quickly concluded by their mouths agape that they very well could. Tony whispered, "Is that the priest from our church when we were little?"

"I guess you all can see him, huh?"

Dursky rolled down his window as if it would give him a better view. Billy could tell instantly that he was now a believer and that there was a very strong chance he always would be. Father Joseph and Andrew made their way up to the steps of the church summoning the power from their protector and savior. They looked like they almost pushed a power through the air. The light began to grow blue again. Those in the car covered their eyes trying to protect them but it still made its way through the protection of their hands and forearms trying to cover them. The car shook and pieces of the dead began to rain down on top of the car.

When the light dissipated Billy opened his eyes to see the dead were gone, and the humans who'd been taken over were out for the count on the ground. Billy squinted waiting for them to come back but the two only stared at each other motioning for the others in the car to come forth. When they did Joseph said, "There is something dark still within the church."

Billy followed behind the two holy ghosts. They got to the door, finding it locked, which didn't necessarily surprise Billy given there were demons and zombies from hell trying to enter the church. Billy brought out a key but there was something keeping the knob from opening. Dursky pulled his revolver firing off three shots into the bottom hinge of the door and three into the top. The rounds tore through the wooden door and when he yanked it again it finally gave enough that they could pry it down off its frame.

They entered the church looking around for James. Billy wanted to scream but was unsure if it was a possibility. When they entered the main hall, they found James and Father Michaels or what was left of him. Billy felt a knife of pain, guilt, and loss running through his heart. Father Michaels lay on the floor, hands outstretched like he died trying to catch himself and the side of his head had been blown off. Tony tried to run but Billy took hold of the back of his jacket yanking him backwards off balance. James looked up to them shaking his head, unsure what else to say. Billy screamed, "What happened, what are you doing, James?"

James stood slowly, keeping his hands away from his sides. The draped curtains moved and Jack stepped out from the shadows of it. He had a silenced pistol raised and pointing at the back of James' head. Billy stopped walking forward, feeling like this might be the end. His faith was seriously being tested, he wondered why God being almighty had not stepped forward. The two ghosts rushed at him and Jack was blind to the fact that they were there. When they tried to pull the demon from his body they stopped, looking back at Billy shrugging as if there was nothing he could do.

Jack said, "If you brought holy rollers here they aren't going to do anything. Satan has promised me everything if I kill all of you and there are only two of you left!"

The list of young and old demon hunters ran through Billy's head. James had already heard the news earlier from him as he tortured and beat Father Michaels making sure that all of the information he needed had been gathered before killing him. Jack cocked the pistol aiming it point blank at the rear of James' skull walking forward until he made the tip of the barrel disappear in his hair.

"You don't want to do this," Billy pleaded.

"You are right, I don't but I don't have any choices in the matter. It is better to have an invitation by your maker than to be forced to go there," Jack said, looking like a psychopath.

"Just don't do anything stupid!" Dursky yelled.

James was slowly moving his hands to his pockets, hoping that Jack wasn't seeing what he was doing. He winced when he smashed the balls of water in his hand. The glass shattered quietly and his blood mixed with the holy water. He waited until Jack was looking at the rest and brought his hand up and his head to the side, making the barrel move out of the way. James screamed, "Go back to hell, demon!" as he let the water go free into his face.

Jack yelled, but only out of annoyance. "What the hell did you throw at me, you idiot?"

"It was holy water, you barely flinched," James stammered.

"I'm not possessed you moron. Free will is what I have and Satan just gave me a choice, an advanced warning of the things to come. Hell is going to take things over and there won't be any need for demon hunters because there won't be any holy to worry about saving when he's done. So, your ridiculous water won't do anything for me! All your other priests are dead. To put it lightly it has been a busy last couple of days."

Billy said, "You killed all of them?" He looked to James, who was holding his hand that was now bleeding.

Jack stepped forward, bringing the pistol up to the back of James' head again. Dursky screamed at the top of his lungs holding his hand behind his back. Jack sighed in annoyance. "You must not be listening to me, that stupid water isn't going to do a damn thing, you freak!"

Dursky smiled, pulling the barrel of his revolver up aiming it at Jack's head and pulled the trigger a single time. The gun barked once, echoing through the church making each person's ears ring instantly. Jack's head snapped backwards and he stumbled into the pew. The statue of Mother Mary dripped with his brains and pieces of his skull to the ground. Relief and sorrow filled their hearts as they walked up looking down at Father Michaels, all of them but Dursky felt like they had lost a piece of their soul.

Dursky walked over stripping the pistol from him and checked his sides seeing that they were filled with gold coins. He looked at the back of them seeing the devil's face on them and on the front the fire of hell was embossed. Dursky hobbled to the pew sitting down, shaking his head at the day that they'd had. He asked quietly, "Is there anything that I can do for you, for any of you?"

They shook their heads slowly. James and Billy walked side by side to Father Michaels' corpse where they knelt and began praying over his body, hoping that they were not too late to give him the prayers that they needed to bless him with. Tony pulled one of his crosses from his jacket and knelt next to his brother and James. The three recited the prayer in unison and they watched as the light came through the window and his soul left his body going to heaven at the invitation of God.

Chapter 21

Two weeks later Parker House

Tony came down the stairs. He'd begun having nightmares again, the ones like when he was a boy. Billy had stayed over trying to help him through his troubles. He and James had been spending every day since trying to come up with a plan. The news about the other priests being murdered for their specific job had done the absolute opposite the devil had wished for. The applications to become a demon hunter apprentice had been overwhelming. James and Billy had begun a training schedule and arranging for the possessed to be brought to their church so that they could first hand give classes and give a solid foundation. The attacks had dried up immediately after Jack had been taken out. Dursky had spent a few days in the hospital properly letting his leg heal or at least begin to heal. Billy had let his hands finally be treated and was the other part of the reason he'd been staying at his mom's place because he looked like he was wearing oven mitts.

Tony made his way into the kitchen. Billy looked up smiling, wondering how he was doing. "You doing any better? I think that you slept at least a few hours last night."

"It feels like I am six again, Billy. I hope it doesn't take years to get back to normal again."

"You weren't ever really normal, Tony, I think you forget that I've known you your whole life. I think there is something here that you might want to take a look at."

Tony pulled a coffee cup down and filled it. He sat down at the table looking up at his brother's very serious face when he opened the diocese's envelope seeing the words, we happily accept you into the church priest's program, congratulations Anthony Parker.

The End

Written by Mike Evans

A quick note from the author, if you enjoyed this book I would very much appreciate you taking a minute to head to Amazon to review this book, or at the least give it a star rating please.

Please see next page for additional info by Mike Evans

Mike Evans Fan Club Page Facebook
https://www.facebook.com/groups/1523345561293296/

Discover other titles by Mike Evans visit

http://www.amazon.com/Mike-Evans/e/B00IQ9Z75A

Books by Mike Evans

<u>The Orphans Series</u>
The Orphans: Origins Vol I
Surviving the Turned Vol II (The Orphans Series)
Strangers Vol III (The Orphans Series)
White Lie Vol IV (The Orphans Series)
<u>Civil War Vol V (The Orphans Series)</u>
<u>Divided Vol VI (The Orphans Series)</u>

Gabriel Series
Gabriel: Only one gets out alive
Pitch Black (Gabriel Book 2)
Body Count (Gabriel Book 3)

<u>The Uninvited Series</u>
The Uninvited Book 1
The Stranger Book II of The Uninvited series
The Unwelcomed Book III of The Uninvited Series

Buried: Broken oaths

Voices in My Head

<u>Demons Beware</u>
Demons Beware Book 1
Deliver Us From Evil Book II of Demons Beware

Deal With the Devil

Zombies and Chainsaws

Dark Roads Book II of Zombies and Chainsaws